The author was born on the lower southwest coast of Florida. He was educated at Everglades City, Florida, until his expulsion from the eleventh grade, at which time he joined the U.S. Navy at seventeen years of age.

Everglades City, the gateway to Florida's 'Ten Thousand Islands,' and more recently known as the marijuana smuggling capital of America, took a toll on the author. Sentenced to three concurrent thirteen year terms in federal prison, he never quit fighting his conviction of guilt by association.

Drawing on his life experience and imagination, the author, a 'Last Florida Cracker,' sincerely hopes his efforts are enjoyed by those who read these pages.

EVERGLADES OUTLAWS

EVERGLADES OUTLAWS

Robert V. Griffin

Copyright © 2003 by Robert V. Griffin.

Library of Congress Number: 2003094530
ISBN : Hardcover 1-4134-1906-2
Softcover 1-4134-1905-4

All rights reserved. No part of this book may be reproduced or transmitted in any form or by any means, electronic or mechanical, including photocopying, recording, or by any information storage and retrieval system, without permission in writing from the copyright owner.

This is a work of fiction and any resemblance to actual events, places, or persons is entirely coincidental. All rights to reproduce this work are retained by the author, *Robert V. Griffin.*

Any non-authorized reproduction by any means is prohibited without written permission of the author.

This book was printed in the United States of America.

To order additional copies of this book, contact:
Xlibris Corporation
1-888-795-4274
www.Xlibris.com
Orders@Xlibris.com
19163

This composition is dedicated to my parents.
They were my rock all the way.

Forward

This is a fictional attempt to portray a part of the outlaw world that includes four generations of lawbreakers in one form or the other. However you may feel about outlaws, they are a part of the world we all live in. Some of them are forced by poverty and circumstances to choose the outlaw trail, and a famous quote once stated, "There but for the grace of God go I."

The Author.

Friend there is a thin line
You might never see
Right where you are standing
Between you and me.

No one loves a loser
But sometimes you can't win
And friend that line between us
Is sometimes very thin.

If you are feeling judgment
Against your fellow man
Look into your mirror
See just where you stand.

Friend that line is thinner
Than you think it could be
One mistake, you could fall
Across that line with me.

I am here in prison
For what I shouldn't do
And there is just a thin line
Between me and you.

Everglades Outlaws

Everglades outlaws blue light law saw
In the sawgrass sliding past
Airboat headlights in the dark nights
Everglades outlaws running fast

Broke the law for our pay
Swamp water everyday
Gator hides for the leather trade

Then they passed another law
Busted everyone they saw
Selling products alligators made

Everglades outlaws blue light law saw
In the sawgrass sliding past
Airboat headlights in the dark nights
Everglades outlaws running fast

Lovely ladies fashion blooms
Fancy hats and feather plumes
Yesterday's Everglades outlaws

Then when Prohibition came
Running rum was the game
Everglades was the name to call

*Whiskey money was long gone
When a state law came along
Salt mullet crossed the Georgia line*

*Marijuana broke the law
Another product all they saw
Easy money made another time*

*Everglades outlaws blue light law saw
In the sawgrass sliding past
Airboat headlights in the dark nights
Everglades outlaws running fast*

*We never though we could fall
Ever land behind the wall
A way of life was over for us all*

*We lived it loose and lived it fast
We never knew it was the last
Days for the Everglades outlaws*

LAST FLORIDA CRACKER

Blue waves washing over
Snow white Florida sand
Old green jungle cover
Fighting for the land

Now a new equation
Changing status quo
Progressive modern nation
Watching Florida grow

New laws unforgiving
For a modern man
Different rules for living
He can't understand

His whole culture leaving
Fading from the scene
He is still believing
But he is just a dream

Last hunter of the wood
Last fisher of the sea
Last time living good
Last cracker living free

Last Florida cracker
Running out of time
His future looking blacker
The last of his kind

Prologue

In the year 1865 the American civil war had ended. Veterans of that deadly conflict were returning to their former homes all over America to try to resume their lives. Some of those veterans from the south would find their homes in ashes, and Union troops occupying their homeland.

Standing five foot ten inches tall and weighing one hundred eighty pounds, with swarthy good looks, James Robert Taylor was one such veteran. James was fortunate in that in spite of being actively involved in many battle actions of the war, he was only wounded one time. At the Battle of Bull Run in the month of August, 1862, James took a flesh wound through the calf of his left leg. He fought bravely for his cause all through the terrible battles of America's greatest test of endurance as a nation.

When the South surrendered to the North on April 9, 1865, James rode south to Georgia. He was sickened by the destruction seen as he rode through the countryside of the Southland. He was more shocked by the destruction of his hometown of Atlanta, and vowed he would ride south to search for his future and make his mark in the world.

CHAPTER 1

James was the bastard child of the wild son of one of Atlanta's most prominent pre-war families. His father's parents were old Yankee lace Irish from Boston's Back Bay upper class. The O'Neils returned to Boston with James' father, their only son and the apple of his mother's eye. James' father was one of those handsome rogues that capitalize on their power over the opposite sex and then move on to other pastures. Such men move through life reaping beauty's bounty and never know or care of the offspring of such idle dalliances.

James' father knew of him but, bowing to family wishes, he abandoned the pregnant woman to her fate. James' mother found work as a seamstress in a garment factory. James Taylor never knew Joe O'Neil was his father. His mother kept her family name of Taylor. She loved and provided for James in the one room shack where he was born in abject poverty on a cold winter morning in 1845.

James was a handsome child with the black hair and blue eyes of the father he would never know. When he was nine years old, his mother died of consumption and a weak heart. James was committed to the county orphanage until he could be adopted, but no one ever did. At the age of thirteen, he was apprenticed to a kind local merchant in the mercantile business. He liked his employer, and worked hard to learn everything he could about the business. When the War Between the States broke out, James enlisted with his employer's blessing and rode north to fight with his regiment.

A sixteen year old boy rode north to fight that summer of 1862, and a twenty year old man rode in defeat through the ruined streets of Atlanta one early morning in 1865. As he rode along James concluded that any future he might have had in Atlanta was gone up in flames with General Sherman's march through Georgia, dealing death and destruction in his path. James thought then of his vow to search to the south for his destiny. One thing he knew was that he was sick and tired of cold weather. He thought then of the land he had heard of that lay to the south, where the weather was warm year 'round and the living was good. The war had hardly touched south Florida and James decided that was where his search would end in happiness. Making up his mind, James rode south out of Atlanta and camped that night by a small creek just off the road a ways.

Early the next morning James saddled up and rode down the road, always riding south. Soon the sun overhead let him know it was noon, and his stomach agreed. He started looking for a place to rest and eat. He saw a little clearing east of the road and another stream of clear running water. James sat smelling the pine scented breeze blowing gently on face. He dismounted and unsaddled his horse, and staked him out to graze on the sweet green grass growing in the little meadow clearing by the stream. James unpacked his saddlebags and built a small fire. Then he walked over to the stream and filled his coffeepot up and put it on the fire. James was slicing up bacon to fry when he noticed his coffee water was boiling. He dumped coffee in the water and then fried cornbread cake and bacon. Lying back resting in the grass James thought, what a life. Quiet and peaceful with no gunfire or war in his life. After about an hour's nap he packed up his supplies, saddled up his horse, and rode on down the road.

Coming around a bend in the road about two hours later, James came up on a wagon turned upside down in the middle of the road. Riding closer James saw the team was dead. Then he saw the body of a young woman lying by the side of the road. He dismounted his horse and knelt down to look at her. Her head was at an odd angle and she had evidently broken her neck in the fall.

At the sound of gun shots in the distance James jumped to his feet, ran to his horse, and stepped up into the saddle. Listening, he heard more shots to the east and he rode in that direction. As he rode closer to the sound of gunfire he dismounted, and creeping through the trees, he tied his horse to a tree trunk. As he peeped though the bushes James counted four men to his right, firing at one man returning their fire from behind a log.

As James watched, one of the four headed in his direction, trying to flank the lone gunman pinned down by the other three. James thought about the scene he was observing and decided that he would help the lone gunman. Making up his mind, James stood up and shot the flanking gunman dead. The other three were looking in his direction dumbfounded. Then they started firing at James. Suddenly the lone gunman stood up and shot one in the head, killing him instantly. James shot another one down, and then the other one cleared out of there on the run.

Coming out in the open, the lone gunman and James started walking toward each other. When they were a few feet apart, James saw a tall handsome blondhaired man grinning with his hand out to him. As they shook hands the man said he was sure glad to see him.

James smiled and said he was always for the underdog, and besides, he had seen the wagon wreck. "Sir, my name is James Taylor. Who might you be?" James asked.

"My name is Ralph Williams," the other man replied. Then he stared off in the distance for a moment. With tears in his eyes he told James that the dead girl was his wife.

They had run off and gotten married over the objections of her family. He told James that his wife's older brother had jumped on him and that he had accidentally killed him in the fight. The whole clan of his wife's people had sworn revenge, and Ralph had fled south with his young wife. After running all night her kin had caught up with them the following day. They shot one of the horses and upset the wagon, killing the other horse. Ralph's wife was thrown and her neck was broken in the fall, killing her on the spot. Ralph picked up his rifle and ran for his life through the woods. Riding up to the wagon and seeing their sister dead, her kin rode after Ralph with murder in their hearts. Shortly after, James came riding down the road and came upon the scene.

Two months later James and Ralph were riding into Tallahassee, Florida. They were worn out and watching their back trail. Ralph knew that his dead wife's kinfolk would never stop looking for them. James thought they would be safe across the state line in Florida. The two men made camp about dark outside of town. After they had eaten their supper Ralph told James that he would like to ride into town, look around, and maybe get a beer. James agreed and they mounted up and rode into town.

Riding down the main street they came upon a small saloon. They tied up the horses to the hitching rail in front and walked inside. Pausing at the door, the musty smell of stale beer and unwashed bodies assaulted their nostrils. They walked up to the bar and ordered two beers. Standing at the bar they glanced around the room at the crowd of men socializing for the evening.

Two men were sitting over at a corner table engaged in a game of checkers. Suddenly one of the men jumped to his feet and said, "You're a damn liar! It was my move and I ain't taking it back!"

The other one said, "The hell you ain't!" and knocked the first one down with his fist. They scuffled around on the floor and hit each other for about four of five minutes. After a while they quit and lay back panting to catch their breath. Then they got up, walked to the bar, and ordered two shots of red whiskey and two beers. Drinking their shots down they stood side by side sipping their beers. Finally one told the other that he was tired and they had to work early the next day. The other man agreed with him, and finishing their beers, they walked out the door together.

"That is about the damnedest thing I have ever seen in my life," Ralph said.

An older man having a beer close by them laughed and said, "Fellers, them two boys is brothers. They have been playing checkers in this town for years and as far as I know they have never finished a game."

James allowed, "It sure was some sight to see." The older man introduced himself as Irving Ledbetter and asked if they were new in town.

"Yes sir, we sure are," James said. Mr. Ledbetter asked them if they were in the market for a job and told them he could sure use some help on his farm. James said to let them talk it over and they would let him know.

James and Ralph moved over to the corner of the room and discussed Mr. Ledbetter's job offer. They decided that they needed a place to lay low for awhile, and they could sure use the money. They walked back to the bar, and James said, "Mr. Ledbetter, you got yourself some hands. When do we start?"

Mr. Ledbetter replied, "Right now, boys, if you want to. I'm fixing to leave for home now." They agreed that they would go break camp and go to Mr. Ledbetter's farm that night. Mr. Ledbetter gave them directions to get to his farm, and they rode into his yard that night and settled into his bunkhouse.

James and Ralph had been with Mr. Ledbetter over five months. The food was good and so were the wages. Mr. Ledbetter was a fair man and a good farmer. There was a little country village store close by and James and Ralph went there to trade. They figured they would keep their supplies stocked up in case they had to move on in a hurry.

The weeks and the months rolled by, and the boys decided that they needed to have a little fun. They told Mr. Ledbetter that they needed some town life for a change.

"Well, boys, you have sure been good help and I hate to lose you, but I know young men have to have a little fun." Mr. Ledbetter paid them their wages, and they loaded up their bedrolls and saddlebags and rode out.

Later that night after an enjoyable evening at Miss Flo's sporting house they tied up at the hitching rail of the Red Dog Saloon. As they walked into the saloon doors, two men at the bar turned and shouted, "There they are!" They both pulled their pistols and started shooting at them.

Ralph was hit in the side and fell to his knees. James pulled his pistol and shot one dead. The bullet hit him square in the face. He shot the other one in the arm and he fell up against the bar. Pulling Ralph to his feet they ran out the door, mounted their horses and rode out, with the other man firing wildly at them from the door.

Two days later they were still riding south. Ralph's wound in his side was clean through, no internal damage or broken bones. James had cauterized the wound and bandaged his side. Ralph told James that he knew the two men in the saloon were not the only ones looking for him. He told James that they would also be looking to kill him too. He had killed three members of their family and wounded two more. His wife's kin were hill folks and they believed in the feud code. There would be cousins and kinfolks that wanted them dead.

Ralph told James that he thought he knew of a place their hunters would never find them. He told James that he had heard of a place on the southwestern coast of Florida that sounded like a paradise to him. James said it sounded like the place he had been told of himself and that was where he was headed when he met Ralph. They agreed it sounded like the place to go, and they rode on south in the night.

Chapter 2

It is summer time in 1874 on Marco Island, south of Tampa on the Gulf of Mexico. Marco Island that summer was a poor man's paradise of a simple life fishing, hunting, and farming the fertile land. Skeeters were put up with by the locals and sand flies were avoided whenever possible. The waters teemed with seafood of all kinds and across the channel were deer and turkey for the taking. The people ate gopher turtles and the seacow was harvested for the table pride. The meat was so good to the natives. They also turned loggerhead turtles for their meat and dug up the eggs to eat. All a store was good for were for the goods that were shipped in that were necessary to live. The native people that had settled along that lower Florida coast helped each other, worked hard, and lived a simple, free life. A few Seminole indians poled their dugout cypress canoes from the mainland to trade. They sometimes brought deer and turkey to trade for their needs. They caused no trouble with the island folks and no one bothered them. Everyone coexisted peaceably.

Ralph and James worked their way south down the coast from Tampa to Marco Island on a schooner. They had sold their gear and horses in Tampa for a fair amount of money. When they sailed into the bay of Marco Island they went ashore with the captain. When they landed on the shore they took their pay and stayed on the island when the schooner sailed out of the bay to the Gulf of Mexico.

The next few years they spent hunting and trapping in the local area. They avoided any strangers that came to the island and believed they were safe at last. They knew that Ralph's wife's kin had gotten the law after them, as well as still hunting them themselves, too.

They both married local girls on the island, and a year later James was the proud father of a son he named Samuel, after a friend killed in the war. Samuel grew to young manhood and learned to be a good hunter and fisherman. Living from the bounty of that wild and beautiful country that was southwest Florida in the late 1800's, he was a happy young man.

James and Ralph over the years were closer than brothers and partners in every venture they entered into. Ralph had woodworking skills, and he and James built a fifty-foot sailing schooner to trade up and down the coast. They prospered very well in the trading venture, making many trips to Key West with fresh vegetables, fruit, and other goods they brought from Tampa. They never stayed in Tampa very long, always leaving as soon as their business was done and on the first tide.

James and Ralph had been in Key West two weeks and their schooner was loaded with goods for the trip home to Marco. They had been waiting for the weather to calm down in the gulf. It had been storming for over a week and they were anxious to get under way and sail for home. Finally the rain stopped and the sun came out. It was a beautiful day in late September and a soft wind from the south brought them out of the harbor, headed north in the gulf for home.

James and Ralph were in their late thirties, strong and healthy men in their prime. Watching their stern on the second day out of Key West they could see that a strong front was building up, that they had noticed on their first night out. Now on their second day the sea was really starting to roll. Huge waves were building up and breaking over the craft. They tied everything down and checked that the hatches were tight. Ralph hollered over the roar of the wind to James, "I believe we got a hurricane coming up now!"

"Me too," James replied. "Let's get most of the sail down and try to head into the shoreline and ride it out." The wind howled and the gulf rose over them, wave after wave. The two friends held onto the wheel and fought the storm together. They saw the shoreline ahead a few miles away.

Ralph said, "I think we're going to make it now, partner."

James said, "Not this time, old friend, look out there." Ralph looked behind and a look of wonder crossed his face as he saw the tidal wave coming at them. James said, "Well, it looks like our run is over now, old pard."

Ralph smiled and said, "It's been a good run, my friend."

They clasped hands and stood tall together looking up at the mountain of water that took them to eternity.

CHAPTER 3

James Taylor's widow never got over losing him to the hurricane of 1879. She died the next August of 1880. Samuel stayed on Marco Island for another year before he made plans to leave the island. The memories there were more than he could bear. His daddy and Uncle Ralph (he called Ralph "Uncle" although they weren't really kin) had been his friends and their loss hurt him deeply.

Sam had been courting Sarah Mills since the fifth grade and loved her with all his heart. He asked her to marry him that September. Sarah had loved Sam for years and she said, "When do you want to, Sam?"

"The first of the month," Sam answered.

They made a nice looking couple as they stood up together the first of October to wed. Sam was tall and blond with his daddy's blue eyes. Sarah was small and shapely with almond shaped brown eyes and her hair was a rich chestnut color. Uncle Ralph's widow, Aunt Esther, cried at the wedding. When Sam told her they were planning to leave the island, she cried again. They both promised her that they would come back for visits often.

The weeks passed and Sam made his plans to leave. Then one day he carried them out. He sold everything, the old home place and all. Then one morning he and Sarah loaded her things onto his schooner. He tied his skiff boats loaded with nets and supplies behind and they sailed south down the gulf coast.

Moving slowly down the coast they fished and hunted plume birds for their feathers, to sell and put money away for a rainy day. They had no need to live in town. The country provided everything they needed except for a few items. Once a year they left their camp and sailed into Key West for supplies that were necessary. Sam bought enough ammunition to last him for many months. Sarah bought thread, cloth, and other things she needed.

They had no children and they accepted that they would probably not have any. Their months passed into years lived happily together in their paradise. Sam would go into the Everglades sometimes for weeks to hunt, and Sarah always went with him. Together they were a team. Sarah was almost as good in the woods as Sam and he acknowledged she was a better rifle shot.

One day word from a passing fisherman informed them that Aunt Esther had died that fall. Sam had loved her very much, and regretted not having visited her as he had promised. One morning of October in 1905, Sarah was too sick to get out of bed. When she did get up she was feeling nausea and weak kneed. Sam was worried sick about her, and stayed close to the camp. He had traplines that he worked and he forgot about them to stay with Sarah. Then Sarah told him she was all right, to go see about his traps and don't worry about her.

After a few days Sarah felt a lot better and was herself again. She went about her chores smiling and humming softly to herself. Sam was at the net spread down by the bay when Sarah came walking down the path towards him. As he looked up at her Sam thought Sarah looked different somehow. Then he said, "Honey, I believe you are getting fat."

She laughed and said, "That happens when you are with child, Sam."

Sam stood up and shouted, "We are? Oh, thank the Lord!" Then he walked her back to their camp and tried to get her to lay down and rest.

Sam told Sarah they would go back to Marco to her folks to have the baby. Sarah told him that they would wait until it was almost time before they needed to go back. As the months passed and Sarah grew large and moved awkwardly, Sam asked her if she was ready to go back to Marco now. She said, "Sam, this is only

April. The baby is not due until the last of May; we have time." Sam told her he was worried and he thought they should go now. She laughed and told him they would leave the first of May.

Sometimes nature ignores the best laid plans. It is five o'clock on the morning of May 2, 1906, and Sam is holding his newborn son, Jessie Allen Taylor, and beaming with pride. Their boat is anchored near the mouth of Shark River on the northern side of Cape Sable. Sarah is in her bunk resting from childbirth. Sam delivered his son as Sarah told him what to do. It was an easy delivery for Sarah in spite of being her first. Their son was a fine healthy baby with a head full of chestnut hair and his father's blue eyes. They returned to their camp and Sam started building a cabin while Sarah and the baby slept on the boat.

The years passed along, and the small family was happy. Jessie was growing like a weed. As he grew older he went with Sam like his shadow. When Jessie was eight years old he was with Sam working the trap lines, fishing, hunting and helping with the garden. Sam taught Jessie everything he could learn from the first of his life. He taught him how to shoot his pistol and how to load it. He taught him how to skin and tan the hides of the game they caught in the traps. Jessie had his own knife in a sheath on his belt and he knew how to keep a sharp edge on it. At nine years old he was a skilled woodsman in the wild land of the country. He could pull the cork line on their fishing net and lay it as good as any grown fisherman anywhere. Sam was as proud of him as a father could be.

One day as they walked along checking the traps, Jessie turned aside to relieve himself while Sam walked on down the line. Sam was taking a dead possum out of the trap when a full-grown panther jumped on his back, knocking him down. Sam could smell the rancid breath of the big cat as he snarled and went for Sam's throat. Sam had both arms up behind his neck, trying to protect himself the best he could, as the panther kept biting his arms. Jessie had walked up at that time, drew his knife, ran up and stuck the blade to the hilt in the cat's back. The panther screamed and started turning circles biting and clawing at his back where the pain was. Jessie ran up to Sam and pulled the pistol from Sam's holster, then turned to face the cat. He held the big pistol in both hands as the panther, crazed with pain, came charging at him. Jessie fired and the bullet hit the cat in his left eye, passing through his brain and killing him instantly. The big cat dropped to the ground a foot in front of Jessie, whose eyes were as big as saucers. Sam was trying to sit up, his shoulder and arms in considerable pain. He finally got to his feet and hugged his son to him. With Jessie helping him they managed to get to the skiff boat and Jessie rowed them home. Sarah was at the landing when they tied up. Jessie took the guns and hides they had taken from the other trap lines and went ahead. Sam, leaning on Sarah, followed Jessie up the path to the cabin. "Sarah," Sam said, "he may be only nine years old, but there goes a man. Our son saved my life today."

The years passed along and as the seasons changed Sam and Jessie worked their traps, fished and hunted together. They came home to Sarah's good meals at evening time and their life was full and happy together. One evening, Sam and Sarah were sitting on the little cabin's front porch enjoying the breeze off the bay. Jessie was down at the net spread by the dock, looking out over the bay shining golden red in the setting sun. "Just look at that boy, Sam." Sarah said, "He's a man now."

"Yeah, he sure is," Sam said, "I believe he's stronger than me now." Sam told Sarah he wondered where the years had gone.

"We have been blessed, Sam," Sarah said. Sam just nodded his head, reached over and clasped her hand, and smiled at her in content.

Sam and Jessie had made them a whiskey still, and for the last two years they had been making the best white lightning in all of the Everglades. That winter, Sam left Jessie home to run the trap lines and stay with Sarah while he took a load of whiskey and hides into Key West to sell. The man that bought his hides was in the whiskey business on the side, and he always bought Sam's moonshine for a good price.

There were several men hanging around the front of the store, and Sam noticed two of them paying more than a little attention to him. He was careful about his transactions, but he was sure they had seen him get paid off in the store. As he walked to his boat Sam watched his back trail, but if anyone was following him they were good at it. On the way home he noticed a small boat coming up behind him. As it got closer he looked back and saw the same two men that had been in front of the store watching him. Sam thought to himself that they were probably up to no good. He thought that he might as well meet them now while it was still daylight.

Sam eased his double-barreled shotgun up behind his leg, below the boat and out of sight, with both barrels cocked and his finger on the triggers. Sam waited on them to catch up, and soon they pulled up alongside his boat. There were the same two rough looking men in the boat. The older man smiled with rotten teeth and said, "Howdy, Captain." The younger of the two, with his hand under his shirt, looked at the other man with a toothless smile.

"What can I do for you fellers?" Sam asked.

The older man chuckled and said, "You can just hand over yore money, pilgrim." Then he made a grab for the pistol in his belt. At the same time the younger one came out with his pistol and was lifting it up when Sam blew them out of the boat with both barrels.

Sam looked up and said, "Forgive me, Lord, but you know they asked for it." Sam reloaded and blew the bottom out of their boat.

Two hours later that night Sam was home with his family. Sarah held him close and said, "Don't fret about it, Sam, you did what you had to do. The law don't need to know and the good Lord will forgive you."

Jessie said, "I should have been with you, Pa."

Sam smiled and said, "Next time, son."

That spring Sam told Sarah that he thought Jessie might be sick or something was wrong with him. Jessie no longer laughed as much and was always staring off into the dark from the dock. Sam said he thought the boy might be a little touched in the head sometimes. He just didn't act like the same old Jessie anymore.

Sarah just smiled, caught Sam around the waist with both arms, looked up laughing into his eyes, and asked, "Sam, don't you know what's wrong? Jessie is lonely."

Sam said, "Lonely? He's got us, what do you mean, lonely?"

Sarah said, "He's lonely for life around other people, or for someone special. Can't you see? We have each other but Jessie is alone here and he has needs. We must move back up the coast and let him see other people his own age. It's time he took a wife."

Sam told Sarah he was a blind fool and of course that was the problem. He said Jessie had been asking a lot of questions about towns lately but he hadn't thought anything about it at the time.

Sarah said that they should move back to Marco Island, that she got lonely for her kin sometimes. She knew Sam didn't have any kin there, but she got lonely for hers.

Sam said, "Lord help me, honey, I just never thought. All I ever needed was you and our son." Then he said he had been selfish and dumb, they would move back to Marco and would Sarah forgive him.

Sarah told him there was nothing to forgive, that she loved him and her whole life was being with him, but they all needed a change. Sam reached out both arms and held her close as she leaned into him.

Chapter 4

It is a bright spring day the following year, and Jessie is sitting on Marco beach with his arms around Elizabeth Walker. Liz, as she is called, is about five foot two, with emerald green eyes and jet black hair and curves that intoxicated Jessie. He is in love and so is Liz. They met by accident the day that Jessie and his family first arrived the previous year on Marco Island. That first day on the island Jessie saw thirteen year old Elizabeth Walker in the big store by the dock on Marco River. She was standing by the counter with a licorice stick in her mouth and looking at the new boy in town. Jessie thought she was the most beautiful thing he had ever seen in his life. He had a funny feeling in the pit of his stomach. Liz took the candy from her mouth and smiling sweetly up at him, said, "Howdy." Jessie swallowed a couple of times before he could reply with a choked sounding howdy.

"Y'all just moved here?" Liz asked Jessie.

"Yes, ma'am, just today." Jessie answered. Liz giggled and told him she wasn't old enough to be called ma'am. As she smiled at him he was red as a beet, when Sarah came into the store and walked up to them.

Sarah said, "Well, Jessie, who is this pretty young lady here?"

Jessie blushed and stammered, "uh ma mauh . . ."

Liz just grinned at him and put out her hand to Sarah and said, "Howdy, ma'am, my name is Elizabeth Walker and I'm right proud to meet you." Sarah smiled at the girl and introduced Sam, who had just walked into the store and up to them. Liz smiled at Sam and shook his hand and Sam was lost on the spot. He thought to himself that this was the girl for Jessie and he told her he was glad to meet her and he hoped they would see her again. Then he and Jessie loaded up their supplies on the boat, told Liz goodbye, and headed out down the channel to their camp a couple of miles away.

Sam and Jessie worked hard clearing a few acres inland from the shore and building a two room cabin. Jessie courted Liz and worked with Sam and they prospered in the community.

Three years after he first met Liz, twenty three year old Jessie married his sixteen year old sweetheart. He built a cabin a short distance away from Sam and Sarah. It was 1929, and the world was changing. Sam and Jessie had put a one cylinder gas engine in their boats and life was a little easier for them. They fished their nets up and down the coast and back bays. Jessie and Liz were happy together and he took her with him everywhere he went. Sam had helped Jessie build his own launch. It was a twenty three foot length and six and a half foot beam wide. They bought a second hand engine and built a small cabin and it was complete. Jessie had two sixteen foot skiff boats and two hundred feet of nets in different gauges. Pretty good for a young man in the year of 1929.

The price of fish was at rock bottom, and no one had any cash to speak of. Sam and Jessie made two trips to Cuba to run rum back to the U.S.A. Alcohol was illegal in America and they made some good money doing it. But then some of the smugglers and the Coast Guard started shooting each other, and Sam told Jessie they didn't need money that bad. They decided to leave the temptation of easy money, and live off the bounty of the land.

They packed up their gear, loaded their families, fished and hunted south along the coast much as Sam and Sarah had done years before. The following year on the 12th of October, 1930, In a driftwood shack on one of southwest Florida's Ten Thousand Islands, Liz gave birth to a nine pound baby boy. They named him John Westly Taylor. When he was just a toddler he would follow Jessie around the cabin wearing Jessie's old cap on his little head. Sam started calling him "Cap" and the nickname stuck to him. Sarah told Jessie that little Cap would make his mark in the world one day.

The two families lived day by day and were happy and

contented. As the years passed on, Sam's step grew slower, and one early morning while watching the sunrise from his cabin's front porch, he went to sleep in his rocker and never woke up. They buried him there on a little shell mound in the middle of the island.

Sarah gradually withdrew inside herself for days at a time. She wouldn't leave her home there when Jessie suggested they go back to Marco. She died of grief, they thought, when three years later they put her beside Sam in the little shell mound on their last island home.

Jessie and Liz moved back to Marco Island after the loss of Sarah. They loaded everything they wanted to keep on the boats and went out the pass to the gulf, then they headed north and ran the coastline to Marco Island. They rented a small house with an outdoor toilet, and they caught rain water to drink. It wasn't much, but everybody else on the island lived about the same. Some of the island folks had cisterns built by or under their houses for drinking water, but mostly they all lived about the same.

Jessie worked out from the island fishing the coast and going in the 'glades to hunt gators. He trapped coons in the mangroves and salted mullet for the Georgia markets. Jessie made a living for his family the best way he could. The Great Depression was on in America and the banks had all failed. People all over the nation were going hungry and looking for any kind of work they could find. In the Everglades the Florida crackers and other folks that had drifted into the area lived off what they could provide for themselves.

World War II was in its second year when word was passed to Marco that the lady at the draft board in Snapper Bend wanted to see Jessie. Jessie told Liz that they probably wouldn't take him in the service, because he was a family man and had to support them. Liz agreed, and told Jessie that he had better go down to Snapper Bend and talk to the lady at the draft board. Early the next morning Jessie got ready to go and Liz handed him his lunch pail with fried venison and cornbread. Liz and Cap walked with Jessie down to the shore and waved him goodbye as he went out the pass to the gulf and headed to Snapper Bend.

Jessie tied his boat up at the city dock and walked to the draft board. He told the lady there that he was Jessie Taylor, and he heard that she wanted to see him. The pretty lady smiled at Jessie and said, "I am Helen Coley, and yes young man, I am sorry to have to tell you, but I have to." She told Jessie that the draft board had drawn his name and he had to report to Camp Blanding, Florida, Monday week. She told him that there were several other men that had also been drafted and they would all meet the bus that Monday, and she would have tickets for all of them. She said she hoped they wouldn't keep him, because she knew he was a family man. She said her son was due to be draft age the next year, and as bad as she needed the job, she would quit before she sent him off to war.

Jessie said, "Yes ma'am, I know what you mean." Jesse thanked Helen and told her he would see her on Monday at the bus station. Then he went down to the city dock, untied his boat, and headed home.

That night he told Liz he didn't want to go, but he had to. He told her that he didn't think he would be gone but a week or two, and then they would send him back home. Liz agreed, and she and Cap went with him to Snapper Bend to meet the bus. Jessie hugged and kissed his family goodbye. Liz and little Cap waved goodbye to Jessie with tears in their eyes until the bus was out of sight.

Later that week Jessie was with a group of other men with their hair cut short, being told they were all in the army now. Two days later a tough Yankee drill sergeant was trying to teach them all to march and cussing them for being so dumb. Jessie had never seen such a man. Here he was worried about his family, and putting up with this feller raising all that hell about how a man should walk. Next day Jessie was a hundred miles from Camp Blanding, hitchhiking south on the Tamiami Trail.

Liz had sent Cap to bed and was sitting on the couch in the

front room, reading the Bible by the coal oil lamp. There was a tapping on the door and she heard Jessie call her name. He whispered, "Liz, blow out the light."

She walked over and blew the lamp light out, and Jessie slipped in the door, took her in his arms, and held her tight. She said, "Wait, honey, let me light the lamp."

He said, "Pull the window shades down first, honey."

Liz pulled the shades down and lit the lamp. Then she turned to Jessie and asked did they let him come home. He told her about the crazy sergeant, and that he couldn't stand to be away from her. He had to be home to make a living for her and Cap. Jessie told Liz that he would slip out in the 'glades and hide out for a while and see what happened. Jessie stayed in the house that night and got his things that he needed to take the next day. Liz got his skiff loaded with his traps and supplies, and about twelve that night Jessie looked in at his son sleeping, kissed Liz goodbye, and slipped out to his boat in the night.

After about a month or so, Jessie tied up across the channel and swam the channel to the island and slipped home. Jessie continued to slip home every two or three weeks, and hid out in the swamps. Then, after several months went by and no one seemed to care or be looking for him, he just stayed home. Life went back to normal for the family and Jessie forgot about the army.

There was no law on Marco; the only law was in Snapper Bend, and they only sent a deputy to Marco every once in a while. When the fish warden came around, everybody on the island knew he was coming before he ever got there.

One day two strangers came to the island. They were toting fishing poles, and gear was hanging all over them. They had white sunburn lotion on their noses and all the crackers knew that they were Yankee tourists. They went over to the big store, and asked some of the men standing around where they could find Sam Taylor. They said that he had been recommended to them as a crackerjack fishing guide by a friend of theirs back home in Ohio.

One of the Jones boys said, "Hell mister, Sam Taylor been dead for years, but his boy is just as good as Sam was."

"Does he live here on the island?" the stranger asked.

The Jones boy said, "Yes sir, right down that little trail there by the bay. It's the first house you come to."

The strangers thanked him and walked down the path to Jessie's house. The short one eased around to the back while the tall one knocked on the front door. Liz opened the door and said, "Howdy. Can I help you?"

The stranger asked if Jessie was home and she said, "No sir, he shore ain't."

About that time the man in the back of the house shouted, "Hold it, Jessie! F.B.I.!" Jessie turned around and the short man put handcuffs on him and they walked around to the front yard.

Liz ran up and tried to hug him. The tall man shouted at her to get back away from the prisoner. She stood there crying as they led Jesse away.

They marched him back up the lane, past the big store, and down to the ferry landing. After a while they caught the ferry back across the river to the other landing where they had left their car. They put Jessie in the front seat, while the short one rode in the back. The tall agent turned the car around and they drove out the road to the Tamiami Trail. There they turned left, and drove straight through to Camp Blanding. They drove up to the main office and turned him over to the military police.

The next morning his first sergeant took him out of the stockade and they went in to see the captain of his outfit. The captain was a fair man, and was from Florida himself. Jessie was lucky that he was his captain. He told Jessie to go ahead and sit down in a chair by his desk. Jessie sat down, and the captain asked why did he run off. Jessie told him that he wasn't used to no man cussing the way that sergeant feller did, and that if he stayed he wouldn't put up with it. The captain explained to Jessie that it wasn't personal, and the man did that to all the men to train them to take orders that would save their lives in combat. Jessie said he didn't understand that, but now after the captain explained it to him he reckoned he could put up with it. The captain asked him if anything else was bothering him. Then Jessie told him that he had to make a living for his family, and he had to go back home to do that. The captain told him that he would make twenty one dollars a month and an allotment to have most of that sent home to his family. Jessie said that was a lot of money, and he didn't know about all that.

He told the captain if he would give him another chance, he would make him a good soldier. The captain did give Jessie another chance, and Jessie finished his basic training at the top of his class. Jessie came back to Marco Island on his basic leave in his uniform, with sharpshooter medals and expert marksman on his chest. Liz and Cap met Jessie at the big store and they hugged tight. Then the happy family walked up the path to the little house by the bay.

CHAPTER 5

Cap is sixteen years old. World War Two is over. Jessie sleeps on an island like Sam, but in the South Pacific, on the island called Batan. Liz is living in the town of Snapper Bend. The town is populated by northern retirees, fishing guides, and commercial fishermen. Snapper Bend is south of Marco Island on the coast and reached by the Tamiami Trail. During the closed season for mullet fish the natives smuggle salt mullet to the Georgia markets for what they called easy money. The money was good because the market was illegal. They were only doing the best they could and saw no harm in it.

Liz mourned Jessie and never got on with her life for years after he was killed in action. But eventually she moved on, and started dating a widower from Ohio, Mr. Jack O'Neil. He had a young son named Joe, who was proud of the fact that he was named after his fourth generation grandfather from Back Bay Boston. He always said it was a shame that the family money ran out long before it got to him.

Cap took the yankee boy under his wing, so to speak, and they became close friends. Cap stood up to the island boys who wanted to whip that yankee boy's ass in school. Joe soon made friends with the island boys and went to school in Snapper Bend until graduation. Then he went off to college at Ohio State to study for a career in corporate law.

One weekend his father came up to see him, and they went out to dinner on the second night his father was there. On the way back to the campus a drunk driver ran a red light, hit their car on the driver's side, killing Joe's father instantly. Joe buried his father next to his mother in Columbus and managed to maintain his studies through the last semester.

That summer he went to Snapper Bend to visit. He and Cap went hunting and fishing together a lot that summer. Cap was dating Betty Brown, a pretty young woman they both went to school with. In high school Joe had a crush on Betty, but neither Cap nor Betty knew it.

Cap and Betty were engaged and they were to be married in May. Cap asked Joe to be his best man and Joe said he would be proud to. Cap and Betty were married in the little community church in Snapper Bend, and ran out in a shower of rice from their friends to Cap's boat. They couldn't afford a trip to have a honeymoon so they went down the coast and camped out for a week. Betty said that was all the honeymoon she needed.

They were happy together and they worked hard and saved their money. After a while they had enough saved to put down on a small two bedroom house in town. That winter Liz wasn't feeling well and Cap was worried about her. He and Betty went to her rented apartment and packed her belongings and moved her in with them over her objections. Cap told his mother that she was home and Betty hugged her and told her the same thing. She said she didn't want to be a burden, but they wouldn't take no for an answer.

Liz lived with them four years and she kept getting worse, and real sick the last year. Cap took her to the doctor, and he told Cap his mother was dying of cancer. Cap took her for every treatment he heard of that might help. He borrowed money on his house and boat, and sold his guns. He took her to Miami to the best doctor he could find, but nothing helped. Cap and Betty took it hard when she died. After the funeral Betty held Cap close and told him Liz didn't hurt no more. Cap nodded and wiped a tear with his work-calloused hands. He told Betty she was a good woman, and he loved her so. They held each other close and finally went to sleep.

The medical bills broke Cap and Betty. Betty got a job in the hotel doing maid work, and Cap started listening to some of the other fishermen's talk that he had turned a deaf ear to before. They called it easy money.

Joe O'Neil left Snapper Bend after Cap and Betty were married, and in his own words he tells us what happened next....

CHAPTER 6

My name is Joe O'Neil, and I am back in Snapper Bend for the first time in five years. I walked into the Everglades Bar, pulled up a stool, and ordered a beer. Little did I know of the action taking place in the Everglades as I was driving across Alligator Alley two nights before.

If I did, I would have seen a DC-3 cargo plane flying low across the Everglades and dropping dark oblong objects at intervals, glowing green in the sawgrass. I would have heard the ever-increasing sound of airboat motors and seen the small white lights approaching the green glowing objects. They were headlights on the caps of the men operating the airboats. They flashed by, circled, and slowly pulled up to the green objects. I would have seen two boats close together shine their headlights at the objects, a brown burlap bag with a green light stick taped to it. As one headlight flashed up to the other boat, I would have gotten the shock of my life. My old childhood friend Cap Taylor was standing there looking at the bale of marijuana and grinning.

I, of course, sitting at the bar and sipping my Bud beer, was unaware of those events I had passed by on my trip across the Alley. Looking around the bar I could only see one guy that I had known before. I detested him then and I still felt that way now. His name was Kim Snell. He was a big lard assed bastard that had the reputation of being a two faced son of a bitch that worked for or against the law. Of course, that depended on the money and circumstances at the time.

"Some guy came in here looking for you this morning," Kim said.

"Did he say what he wanted?" I asked.

"I don't know what he wanted, he told me he heard you were back in town and wanted to see you," Kim said.

"What was his name?" I asked.

"You know him from the old days before you left town. It was Cap Taylor," Kim said.

"Yeah, I know him. He's an old friend," I said, "I'll see if I can get up with him."

"Well, I don't know," Kim said, "I wouldn't trust my friends now-a-days."

I just looked at him. "I didn't know you had any," I told him. If looks could kill I would surely be dead. Kim was a jerk, but he was a dangerous guy who would use a knife quick.

"Joe, if it's trouble you're looking for, you have found it," he said.

"Whatever's fair, stupid," I said. With a crazed look in his eyes he had a knife out and was coming at me fast. He held it low with the cutting edge up, and he was coming in fast and low to my gut. But as fast as he was, I was faster. I just stood up and blocked the blade with the stool. The blade stuck in the seat a good two inches. Then I simply spun around on a pivot and cracked him along side his head with the stool He went down and stayed there. My military training paid off, it seems.

"Hey, Tina," I told the bar maid, "tell this jerk I'll hurt him if there's a next time." I turned and walked out to my pickup, got in and drove over to Cap's house. I rang the bell but no one answered, then I saw the note. It had been folded and stuck in the door. It was none of my business, except that Cap had been looking for me, and I thought it might be for me. But the note said, "I was here to see you. I'll be at the Oyster Café later tonight." It was signed "Roy Depeppo." He was a local cop lieutenant with the Sheriff's narcotic team. The Oyster Café was a seafood restaurant in town that had a name for excellent seafood. It was also a hangout for a group of local men that everyone in town was aware of being smugglers.

I wondered where Cap and his wife, Betty, were. It seemed odd that no one was home. Especially since Cap had been hunting me yesterday. There were two daily newspapers in the driveway. I turned away, sticking the note in my pocked without thinking. A car pulled into the driveway and Roy Depeppo jumped out and ran up to the door. He looked all around the front step and on the ground in front of the house. Then he turned and rushed by me to his car.

"Hey, what's wrong?" I asked. "Where's Cap?"

"Don't worry about it, man," he said. Then he got in his car and drove off. Well, I don't know why, but something didn't sit right with me. Roy Depeppo was a newcomer to town and had been pointed out to me. I was back in Snapper Bend for a vacation after five years or so, and he didn't know me at all. Puzzled by his actions, I turned and walked back to Cap's house again.

"What the hell," I thought. Cap's my friend and I've been in his house many times. I tried the door and guess what? It was open. So I just walked right in. At one time Cap and I were close enough that I knew something was wrong here. The kitchen was clean and the beds were made. I was looking around when I heard a car in the driveway. I went to the front room and looked out the window. A girl was coming up to front walk. Quickly I turned and ran to the back bedroom. Peeking out to the front room I saw the front door open and she was a ten on the scale, standing there looking around the living room. She closed the door, turned around and walked right in the bedroom and caught me slipping into the closet. Before I could turn, she had a small caliber gun in my back.

"OK," she said, "just back out of there." She stepped back, still pointing the gun at me. I slowly turned around with my hands up and faced her. "What are you doing in this house?" she asked.

"Well, I am a friend of Cap's," I said. "He left word he wanted to see me, and he said it was important, so here I am."

"Well," she said, "that may be so and it may not. You just back over there and sit down nice and easy and maybe I won't shoot you."

Well I did exactly as she said. I didn't want to see if she would shoot. I never trust an excited beautiful lady with a gun. Then I heard the front door open and two men walked into the room. One I recognized immediately. He was a well known Colombian smuggler named Manny Ochoa. The other man was, guess who? Yeah! That jerk from the Everglades Bar, Kim Snell. You never know which side that scum would show up on.

"What have we here?" Manny asked the girl. The girl, it turned out, was Rita Sanchez. She was a beautiful blonde Cuban girl with incredible blue eyes, and a body like a construction worker's dream. As I said before, she was a ten. It was a shame she was hooked up with these guys.

"When I came in," she said, "he was searching the house. I don't know what for, but I'm sure he has the answer. He says he's a friend of Cap's."

I stood up. "Well, one thing's for sure," I said, "you're sure not Cap's friend, mixed up with these two."

Well, that did it. Old stupid Kim rushed to hit me and knocked Rita aside, causing her to drop her gun. What else could I do? I reached under my shirt, pulled my forty-five out and smacked old Kim in the forehead with it. He went down and I trained my gun on Manny while I scooped Rita's thirty-two up in my left hand. "Now, then," I said, "let me ask some questions. First, girl, why are you involved with these guys?"

Well, I have done some dumb things in my life. When I snatched up Rita's gun and swung around to cover them, my back was to the door. I never heard him until he said, "OK, man, just drop the gun!"

I knew that voice from somewhere, but where? Well, Manny got his gun out and covered me. Then good old Kim hit me with what must have been brass knuks and darkness came.

When I opened my eyes it was still dark. Then after what seemed like hours the room I was in grew lighter with the coming dawn. My hands were tied behind my back and my feet were tied. After looking around I could see I was in some kind of old wooden house on the floor. It seemed like I was in a hunting camp. I rolled over on my stomach and inched my way to one of those old-fashioned portable kitchen cabinets against a far wall. I wiggled around to the side and after many tries I managed to kick it over. Talk about the luck of the Irish. When it tipped over the drawer slid out and dumped on the floor. Spoons, forks, and butcher knives. I won't bore you with the details, but I was soon free and walked outside.

I could see I was on a small island in the Everglades. These are islands of high ground in the rivers of grass and water in the Everglades. They are reached only by airboats or by walking thought the swamps and sawgrass. Airboats are metal or fiberglass sled type boats powered by car or airplane motors with propellers attached and steered by wind rudders. They slide very fast over the shallow water and grass of the vast Everglades west and north of Miami. Smugglers say they use these fast boats to retrieve air drops of narcotics.

As I stood there I heard the unmistakable sound of airboat motors approaching. Quickly I ran inside, grabbed up a butcher knife, and jumped out the back door into the swamp. Turning I slid down in the water and under the house and hid behind one of the pilings. Two boats came into view in front of the camp, slowed down, and gently slid up to the dock. Manny and Kim were in one boat with another man I had never seen before, and the blonde, Rita, was in the other boat.

Manny said to the other man, "Carl, we are going up to the other camp by the Dogleg Canal and see if we can help Cap remember where he hid that load of pot."

Carl said, "Hey Manny, don't mark his old lady up too much; I want to check that out when this is over."

"Hey Carl," Manny said, "you and Rita check on the amigo of Captain Bud and then come on up to the Dogleg."

"OK, boss," Carl said, "we won't be long."

Manny and Kim roared off to the south as Carl tied up to the dock. He and Rita came up to the dock and as Carl held the door for her to step through, I gently eased the butcher knife around with the blade against his throat. He gasped, and when Rita turned around I was holding his gun pointed at her beautiful chest.

"Oh my God," she said, "don't shoot!" and dropped her gun

behind her. I marched them inside, picked up her gun and put it in my pocket. I then told Rita to tie Carl up with my old ropes. After she did I backed her up with a wave of Carl's gun, checked her tie job, and rapped Carl on the head to put him to sleep.

Satisfied, I motioned for her to sit down and I straddled a chair and looked at her. "What am I going to do with you?" I said. "Do I have to tie you up and leave you here too?"

"No," she said, "I think it's time I told you the truth."

"So, tell me the truth," I said.

"I will," she said, "but first I want to settle my mind about you. Just who are you anyway? How do you fit in this picture?"

"Well, Rita, I guess you should know the truth about me. I am a DEA cop. I was working narcotics on the East Coast of Florida and was on a two weeks vacation to my old hometown. Now it seems my work is never done, I'm still on the job."

"Well, I'll be damned," Rita said, "I thought you were a smuggler being friends with Cap and all."

"Well I'm not," I said, "but evidently you are."

Rita laughed and said, "No, honey, I'm DEA and working under cover. Say, what is your name anyway?"

I grinned and said, "My name is Sgt. Joe O'Niel but you can call me Joe." About this time old Carl was beginning to come around from the rap on the head I had given him earlier. So I walked over and tapped him into slumberland again with his own gun. I figured he needed some more rest.

"Well, Rita," I said, "help me gather up all these knives and anything else that old Carl here can cut himself loose with, then we can try to rescue Cap and Betty."

Rita got up and together we checked the cabin over for any other sharp instruments. Satisfied, I checked Carl again and we walked out to the airboat. Well it had been a long time since I had been in this part of the Everglades. But Rita said that the camp we were looking for was north of the Dogleg Bend in the Cypress and on the canal itself. With that information in mind, I thought I could easily find it. I flipped the mag switch on and hit the starter. It caught with a roar and I flipped the other mag in and it leveled off and started running as smooth as silk. The boat was about eleven feet long and powered by what looked to be a Lycoming upstack properly punched out to three hundred. This baby would really run.

We tore out of there like a shot and headed south. When we got to Dogleg, we pulled into the deep canal and turned north. Luckily this particular boat had twin mufflers and the most noise it made was when it was revved up and running on the grass. We just slipped along on idle about five miles an hour and after a while we saw the other airboat tied up at the camp. I slid into the bank about a hundred feet from the camp and tied up.

Rita and I stepped out of our boat into knee deep water in the cypress. We started wading towards the backside of the camp. About halfway there on my right I saw the nose holes and eyes of about an eight foot gator. They say the distance between a gator's nose and his eyes in inches corresponds to feet in overall length. Anyway, Rita saw him and started shaking with fear.

"Will he catch us?" she whispered.

"I don't think so," I said, "but stay close to me and let's try to get by him." I knew he wouldn't do anything unless somebody had been feeding him, and I doubted that out here. But I was saving this "rescue" for favors later on. Sometimes I'm just a slick old dog. We were close enough now to hear voices and what sounded like a slap and a cry.

Gently I pulled myself up on the catwalk, turned and helped Rita up. Looking in the window I could see Cap tied in a straight back kitchen chair. Across to the side I could see Betty tied to another chair. She was crying and her face was red where Kim had been slapping her. Cap was sitting there looking at Kim with a look of pure hatred on his face. According to our plan, Rita went around the catwalk to the north side of the dock as if she had come from the other camp walking.

"Help! Help me!" she shouted. Manny and Kim rushed outside the cabin to the dock.

"Where's Carl?" Manny asked.

"He's hurt!" Rita said, "He flipped the airboat on a stump." By that time I was behind them with Carl's gun trained on them. "Freeze!" I shouted. They froze. Rita, by then, had her gun out and was covering them from the side, giving them no chance to jump her. "Well now, boys," I said, "take those guns out. Now one at a time, and if you try, you die."

Manny lifted his gun out and dropped it. "Now," I said, "take your foot and push it out in front of you. Rita, if Snell there even blinks his eye, kill the bastard." After we had them disarmed I marched them into the cabin while Rita gathered up the guns and came in behind me.

Cap sure was glad to see us as Rita untied him and Betty. "Joe, I'm damn glad to see you, buddy. Where have you been so long?"

"Well, Cap," I said, "it's a long story that I'll get around to telling you, but not now." Slyly winking at Rita and unseen by anyone else I said, "We are making a citizen's arrest of these two, and then you can tell me what brought all this trouble for you and Betty."

After we had tied Manny and Kim up, I searched around and found some coffee. I got the gas stove fired up to boil the water. The girls looked in a cabinet and came up with a can of beef stew and a can of pork and beans. Rita found a tin box of saltine crackers and before long we were eating in style. Manny never said a word. He just sat and stared at us, but Kim Snell was a different story. He started begging for food.

"Can't you give a man something to eat? I'm starving." He said.

"Try living off that blubber and shut your mouth," I said. Both Cap and Betty felt sorry for him and wanted to feed him, but I said, "No, he doesn't deserve anything. Well, Cap, what's been going on with you since I've been gone?"

"Well, Joe, like you said, it's a long story, but you tell me, man, what have you been doing for a living? This is the first time you have been home in five or six years, man."

"Well, Cap, I've been working over on the East Coast around

Ft. Lauderdale climbing poles for Florida Power and Light. This is the first vacation I've had, and I decided to come home. So," I said, "what about you? What have you been doing?"

"Hell Joe," Cap said, "you know about me. I fished all my life, and then them government fellers made that damn park and said we couldn't fish there no more. Then when we just wanted to go in there and camp and catch a few mullet to eat, some damn Yankee park ranger would come run us off and threaten to arrest us. Hell, one of them bastards had himself a map and was still turned around until we showed the dumb son-of-a-bitch the way to the Gulf. Then we figured to hell with it. We can just fish back up home. We did for a few years. But I'll be damned if them hogs decided they was going to protect them some more of the country. Well, hell, they made the whole coast park and off limits to the commercial fisherman from Flamingo plumb to Fakahatchee."

"Cap," I said, "knowing you all these years, I'd better put this talk on hold until we can get these bastards to town, and then we can catch up on the news."

"OK, Joe," Cap said, "I'm ready when you are." So we marched our prisoners out to the boats and took off up the trail to the other camp. We picked up Carl there and then with Cap running one boat and me the other, we ran the trail to Alligator Alley. Manny and Carl told us to go to hell when I asked for the car keys and directions. But after I rapped old Kim on his head lightly, he was a regular tour guide. We slid up to the canal and there on the other side on the shoulder of the road were two Ford Broncos with trailers behind them. Hell, I wasn't about to drag those boats along, so I unhitched the trailers, left the boats, and we took off in the Broncos.

Down the road a big dark car turned around and started blinking his headlights behind us. I pulled over to the side of the road, another dumb move on my part. It was now just first dark and he pulled up behind me wit his bright lights on and walked up to the driver's window, which was me. Cap was in the Bronco ahead. He shined his light right in my eyes and stuck a gun in my ear.

"OK, little lady," he said, "you just move real easy and untie Mr. Ochoa and don't try anything or I'll kill this gentleman and then you, capish?"

"Do it, Rita," I said, "he'll shoot you." That voice again. Where had I heard it before? Strange, I couldn't recall where. Well, Rita turned and soon Manny was loose. He took her gun and got out of the Bronco.

"Now, puta," he said, "turn Carl loose."

About this time Cap walked back. He was blinded by the car lights. "What's going on, Joe?" he asked.

"Just turn around, Cap," Manny said, and Cap stopped.

"Better do what he says, Cap, they got us again." I said.

Manny said, "Come on, Cap, let's go get Kim loose, and you had better hand me that gun." Cap handed over Kim's pistol and again we were their prisoners. After a short conference with the man who I now thought of as "The Voice," we again found ourselves tied up and on airboats headed back into the swamp. How could I be so dumb? I couldn't believe this was happening to me again, and this time we were all prisoners.

Manny left us at the first camp north of Dogleg, and told Carl he damn well better watch us this time. He said that he had to get back to town and he needed Kim to help him when he met some of the guys from Miami. After a quick search of everyone he seemed satisfied and walked out the door. We heard his airboat start up and leave with a loud prop wash behind. Carl came in, looked at us tied hand and foot, seemed satisfied, walked in the other room and lay down on the old couch there.

"I'm tired," he said, "but I can see in there so nobody had better move."

I was lying on my side with my face to the sink. Something was reflecting the light from under the oilcloth that hung down as a curtain in front of the sink. I slowly turned over with my back against the oilcloth. Felling with my fingers, I slowly pulled into my hand something we had missed before. A small paring knife had rolled under the edge of the oilcloth. Again blessing the luck of the Irish, I reversed the knife and cut my hands loose. By then I could hear good old Carl sounding off like a sawmill. Poor old Carl woke up with the paring knife at his throat and his gun in my hand. I moved the knife and motioned him up with the gun.

"Damnit to hell," he said, "Manny's going to kill me."

"Somebody's bound to sooner or later," I said. Now you get into the other room and untie everybody, and no tricks or Manny won't have to kill you." Well here we are again, free and Carl our prisoner once more. We all loaded into the airboat and started up the trail to the landing.

When we slid up to the Alley it seemed our luck had held. One Bronco was there and good old Carl had the key. After tying up the boat we all loaded up into to Bronco and made it to town about daybreak. Just as we came up the main street, having dropped Cap and Betty off at their house, we saw Manny and Kim go by in the other lane, headed east.

I swung by the substation, and Rita and I took Carl in and identified ourselves to the Commander. We left Carl with him, swore him to secrecy, and dashed out to the Bronco.

I made a quick detour by my rental bungalow, a block away, and came out with my war chest. We were back on their trail. Then we almost ran over them when they pulled out of a 7-Eleven and headed north toward Alligator Alley. We stayed behind them, but they must have seen us. They turned right around in the road and came by shooting. I ducked down, lost control of the Bronco and ended up in the ditch.

CHAPTER 7

By the time I got the four wheel drive in and backed out, they were gone. Now, I thought, it's time to go back to Cap's house. When we pulled up to Cap's place I was happy to see my pickup was still at the curb where I had parked it. At least we could have different wheels.

Cap met us at the door and said, "Come on in, Betty's just put on the coffee."

"Well that sure sounds good to me," I said. "How about you, Rita?"

Rita laughed and said, "I'd rather have a hot bath."

Betty smiled and said, "Come on with me Rita. I'll run you a tub and you can have a nice soak while I fix the boys some breakfast, then we can eat later."

They left the room and I turned to Cap and took the coffee he handed me. "Well, Cap," I said, "what's the rest of the story?"

"Joe," he said, "it's the damn Yankees. They come down here and see this country. Hell, it's like nothing they've ever seen before. They don't understand it, but by God they are going to protect it all for the people to enjoy. So they make a park out of it. Then they got them damn rules that don't let you go in there without checking with some fool from New York City or Seattle, Washington somewhere to tell you where you can go in country your great-grandpa fished, hunted, and raised his family in before this was even a county. Joe, it finally got to the point that we couldn't fish the canals, because them Yanks said we kept them up at night. So they got laws now to keep us out from the canals. So I decided to go back to guide fishing parties for sport fish."

"I used to do it, you remember? I was about nineteen or twenty then. Hey, that's about the time you was north in Ohio, huh? Damn, Joe, you was here so long I forgot ya'll was from up North. Anyway, you know what I mean. I ain't cussing all Yanks, just the ones that want to make this country like it was where they came from. All them damn rules and regulations, a man can't breathe for them. Then they hog all the waterfront and fence it off so you can't tie your boat up nowhere without paying one of them bastards. Don't get me wrong Joe, they is some mighty good people from up North and they don't like the change any better than we do. Joe, they's so many fellers trying to guide that there just isn't any money in it anymore. Joe, don't take offense now, but damn if the Yankees ain't took over guiding, too."

Betty came in the living room and told us that breakfast was on the table. Nobody had to tell me twice. I headed for the table with Cap right on my heels. Betty had outdone herself. That table was something to see. She had fried eggs, ham and grits, plenty of butter for those big old cathead biscuits. Man, that woman could cook! Nobody said a word for at least thirty minutes. Finally I sat back, held my stomach in, and smiled at Cap.

"Boy, you sure got it made, Cap." I said.

He just smiled at me and said, "Yep. I got me a good woman and I chased her until she caught me."

Betty came back into the room with Rita and said, "Well at least ya'll left me and Rita a few groceries." Then she looked at Cap and with that sweet smile, said, "Honey, you and Joe go on out on the front porch and finish your talk. Me and Rita will just set here and eat a bite."

Cap chuckled and said, "Come on, Joe, I've been leading up to something that I guess I got to get off my chest. "We went out to the front porch, sat down in a couple of rockers and Cap looked at me and said:

"Hell, Joe, a man can only take so much. I don't know where you stand on what I'm about to tell you. But you're a working man like me. Suppose they outlawed your climbing job with the light company? And then you said to yourself, 'Well, I'll just get to work with the phone company. They got poles to climb.' Well then, suppose they come along and outlawed that too; and everywhere you tried to make a living you was stopped, and you didn't have no learning, and that was the only job you know how to do? Well, then your pockets is empty, your truck payments is past due, there ain't no groceries in the house, and you can't even catch a mess of fish with your net to eat because some feller up there in Washington said you couldn't. Then you listen to what some of the other fishermen say. Joe, I ain't getting rich. Some of the boys has. I'm just trying to have a few of the things what them fellers on the TV says is above the poverty level."

"Cap," I asked, "what in the devil is Manny trying to get you to tell him, that he kidnapped you and Betty for? Why haven't you gone to the police?"

"Joe, I couldn't. It ain't Manny, it's his boss. He is a powerful man."

"Who is he, Cap?" I asked.

"I can't tell you, Joe. It would be worth my life if he found out, and believe me it would be bad for you to know, too. He is a bad man and you are already in trouble. You need to cut your vacation short and get back to your job. Joe, I am your friend and I don't want you to get hurt."

"Cap," I said, "I haven't been entirely truthful with you. I was fired from my job. I had some trouble with my supervisor. He found some pot in my locker and the Union had no choice so they let me go."

"Damn, Joe," Cap said, "maybe I can help you."

"Well, Cap, I've been putting on a good front, but my cash is sure getting short."

Cap thought a while and then he said, "Joe, what do you think about the marijuana business? Think you could do it?"

"Well Cap," I said, "I guess so. I've been smoking it for years and it never hurt me any. What about cocaine? Are you in that too?"

"Hey Joe," Cap said, "I don't mess with that stuff. We just fly the pot in and drop it in the Glades. That's where you come in. You can run one of the airboats and help pick it up."

"Thanks a lot, Cap, this job will be a life saver for me."

"That's all right, Joe," Cap said, "I'm your friend, ain't I?"

"Yes you are, Cap, and a damn good one."

"Well," Cap said, "you just go over to that fancy place you got rented and get your things. You can stay here with Betty and me. I know you can't afford to be over there."

"Cap, you are something else. I don't know what to say."

Cap just sat there and grinned at me and rocked back and forth in his chair.

"Say Cap, I been meaning to ask you about Rita."

"Well Joe, there's not much to tell. She came over here from Miami with Manny Ochoa and I guess they fell out. But she and Betty hit it off pretty good. I think she is a decent girl. She sure is pretty, Joe, and I think she likes you."

Well, I smiled and thought, now I know why Rita thought I was a smuggler, when she found out Cap and I were friends.

Betty walked out on the porch and said, "Cap, do you think it would be all right if Rita could stay with us for a while? She's afraid of Manny now."

"Sure, Honey," Cap said, "we have plenty of room, and Joe will be staying here too."

Betty smiled at me and said, "Rita will like that, I think."

I just grinned at her. Betty turned and walked back in the house and Cap said, "Well, partner, you all set, huh?"

"Sure am, Cap." I said, "You're a real pal. Say, Cap? Now that you and I have been honest with each other, what's your problem with Manny and The Voice?"

Cap said, "The Voice?"

"Well," I laughed, "that's the name I gave the man who keeps slugging me and sticking guns in my ear. I call him The Voice because I never see him, but I've heard that voice before; I just can't place it."

"Oh!" Cap said, and resumed his rocking. "Well, Joe, about me and Manny. He is one of the guys from Miami that I contract to pick up their loads and stash them in the swamp until they come for it. Then we take airboats and bring it to the Alley to them. Then they haul it off and sell it, I guess. I don't know about that end of the business. Anyway, someone found the stash and stole it, and Manny thinks I'm lying and stole it myself. But I didn't, Joe. I think his right hand man Kim Snell stole it. He's a sorry bastard and always was since the first day he came over here from Miami. I never did like that feller."

"That makes two of us, Cap," I said, "I don't like him either. Well listen, Cap, I have a few things to do in town and then I might run over to Lauderdale and pick up the rest of my stuff. I'll see you when I get back."

I went and told Betty goodbye and asked Rita to go with me. So Rita and I left Cap's house in my pickup. We drove over to the Sheriff's office and found the same watch commander on duty. He took us in his office and assured us that our cover was secure, and that he had Carl safely tucked away and held on supervision. "Well, Commander," I told him, "it looks like we have gained the trust of some of the local smugglers. We need to keep this cover for a while."

"Don't worry," he said, "it's safe with me." We got up and shook hands with him and left.

"Well, Rita, what do we do now?"

"I don't know, Joe, I guess we have to find Manny and Kim."

"I guess so," I said, "but where? Listen Rita, Manny thinks you have double-crossed him, right?"

"Yes," she said, "and he thinks you are a smuggler just like I did."

"Well," I said, "what could be better? We will let him keep on thinking that." We drove around town for a while, then I decided to go back to Cap's house. We pulled into Cap's driveway and Cap met us at the door.

"Go on in, Rita," he said. "I want to have a few words with Joe, OK?"

"Sure, Cap," she laughed, "I know you guys have your little secrets just like us girls." Cap just smiled that old slow grin at her as she went into the house.

"Take a seat, Joe," Cap said as he sat back in his rocker.

"What's up, Cap?" I asked.

"Well, old buddy," he said, "tonight you are going to fatten that billfold of yours. I just got word that we got a little pop-up job that no one else can handle right now."

"That sure sounds good to me, Cap," I said.

"Well, Joe," Cap said, "I sure had a hard time convincing the boys that you're OK. I put my name on the line and told them how we have been friends for years, and they finally came around."

That night, Cap took me with him in his pick-up to a rendezvous with his crew. "Come on with me, Joe," he said.

Everybody loaded up in a van type panel truck, and we drove for about an hour on the main highway. We turned off onto a dirt road and after about twenty minutes we stopped. A guy came up to the window of the van on Cap's side and said, "Hello, Cap."

Cap answered, "How's it going, Ricky?"

"Pretty good Cap. The shrimper is on the way in now."

Cap already knew it. He had been on the VHF with the pick up boat the last two minutes. "Fine, Ricky," Cap said, opening the door and getting out, "OK, boys, let's go make up some money."

Everyone unloaded from the van. I could see that we were in the mangroves on the edge of a newly platted subdivision with no noticeable development. We were parked by a creek in a clearing. The creek ran into the bay. From the Gulf of Mexico through a pass the shrimp boat would come into that bay. Then small fishing boats known as "well boats" would come out to unload the bales of pot. They were called well boats because the outboard motors were situated in a well in the front third of the boat. This leaves two-thirds of the boat space wide open to hold a net for fishing. In the old days they were referred to as mullet skiffs. Of course, in this case the load was pot.

In about ten minutes, one after the other, five well boats came idling up the creek to tie up to the shoreline of the creek. When they had shut their engines down Cap said, "Well boys, she's on the way in. We got about fifteen minutes. Now I want you boys to decide who wants to go out and who wants to load the trucks."

"OK, Cap," one man said. Then they grouped up to decide among themselves.

"How much we got coming, Cap?" one man asked.

"About twenty three thousand, Johnny," Cap said.

About that time a voice came over Cap's radio. "Coming in the front yard now, Six Pack."

Cap said, "Yeah, I gotcha there, Saltwater." About that time a big loadstar diesel truck pulled into the clearing. Then in a couple of minutes another straight twenty two foot box loadstar pulled in and parked behind the other one. Then another big box truck pulled in and parked. It was a well known rental truck. Cap walked over to the last truck and talked to the driver for a few seconds. Then he turned around and said, "OK, boys, let's get 'er done."

I got on the front well boat with Cap and the unloading crew got on the rest of the boats. A few men stayed behind to load the trucks that were turning around and getting into position. Then we were out of the creek and into the bay.

Cap's radio came on. "Sixpack, Sixpack, over."

Cap answered, "I see your light, Saltwater, about five more."

"Gotcha, Sixpack."

In about five minutes we pulled up beside a seventy five foot shrimp boat. There was no running tide and the bay was calm as a lake. We tied up and the rest of the boats came by, unloaded their men on our well boat and then up on the shrimp boat.

"Howdy, Sam," Cap said, "glad to see you."

"Proud to be here, Cap." Sam said. "We was sure lucky to get though the gap this time. We saw a cutter but they didn't pay us no mind. Boy, I tell you my ass was tight for a while there."

"I know what you mean, Sam." Cap said. "OK, boys, let's get that ice hole open and get to work, we got a lot to unload. We don't want daylight catching us here."

The men pulled the hatch cover off the hole and two of them started passing bales out to the rest of us. We in turn passed them over the side and down to be loaded on the well boat. Soon it was loaded and left for shore and another pulled into place and it was loaded. By the time we got the last one loaded the first one was back for another load. I was amazed at the efficient way these simple fishermen coordinated their work. Soon our well boat was the last of the load. We had unloaded the forepeek and ice holds in record time.

Cap turned to the pick up boat captain and said, "Jerry, after you lead Sam back out I want you to follow him on out and pick him up."

"What's up, Cap?" Sam asked.

"Well, boys," Cap said, "this boat's been on the hot list, I don't know how come it ain't been caught. You boys take her out to about fifty feet of water and open the seacock. Stay with 'er till she goes down, then haul ass to the house."

"OK, Cap, you got it." Sam said.

We crawled over the side to the well boat and headed to the creek with the last of the load. Looking back I could see the big shrimper headed back to the gulf. I thought, what a shame to sink such a nice boat.

Pretty soon we were tied up and unloaded the last of the boatload. By this time the first two trucks were loaded and we finished up the last one. "Alright boys, we done a good night's work." Cap said. "Take a rest for a while."

I was amazed to see that some of them had already gone to sleep. "What are we waiting for, Cap?" I asked.

"Well, Joe, if you was the law you would know why we are waiting." Cap said.

I damn near fainted. If he knows, he will kill me, I thought. "What do you mean, Cap?" I asked.

"Well Joe, wouldn't you think it strange that these trucks would be rolling around town at this time of night?"

"Yeah, I guess I would." I said.

"Well, you worked hard tonight. Why don't you go on and rest a while? We won't be pulling out for a while yet."

"OK, Cap." I said.

"We'll move out about the time all the delivery trucks are starting to roll," Cap said.

"You sure know what you are doing, Cap," I said.

Cap chuckled and said, "It ain't nothing but common sense."

I went over and sat down by one of the guys. He looked at me and said, "Ol' Cap's slick, huh?"

I said, "Yeah, he's slick all right."

The guy looked at me and said, "You done good, Joe. I didn't much want to work with no yankee, but Cap said he trusted you with his life, and that's good enough for me. You done a good job, Joe." He lay back and soon was sound asleep. I lay back and looked up at the millions of bright pretty stars and realized that I felt content and satisfied with a job well done. What a live these people live! They are not mean people just native Florida Crackers, a rare breed of people whose unique way of life as fishermen on this coast of the Everglades is becoming extinct. They automatically cuss everyone from somewhere else as "damn Yankees," then they will turn around and give that same person the shirt off their back if he approaches one of them without being overbearing.

Cap's voice broke into my thoughts and I sat up. "OK boys, load up, it's time to go," he said.

The big trucks pulled out in five minute intervals. We followed the last truck out to the highway. There it stopped and I saw the driver get out and start fooling around under the back of the truck. "What's going on, Cap?" I asked.

"They are hooking the taillights back up," Cap said.

I could see Rick walk out to the highway and flash his pencil light. The truck moved out on the highway, turned his headlights on and pulled away. Our van pulled up to the highway and stopped. Rick came up to Cap's side. Cap said, "You know what to do, Ricky."

"Yeah, Cap, I got my fishing pole on my bike."

"OK," Cap said, "stay out there till good daylight and make sure it's clean."

"You got it, Cap," Rick said, and walked over to the highway and flagged us out.

"Damn, I'm tired, Cap." I said.

"It won't be much longer, Joe," Cap said.

Pretty soon we turned off the highway onto a dirt road leading up to a ranch house set way back from the highway. We came to a gate and Cap got out and opened it. The van drove through, and Cap closed the gate and got back in the van. We drove on about a quarter of a mile and up in back of the ranch house. The trucks were all three backed up to the back door. As we pulled up in the yard one of them pulled out and over to a garden hose and proceeded to wash the back of the truck out. Everybody in the van unloaded and soon we had the other two trucks unloaded. They pulled over to the hose as the other truck left. These men sure know their job, I thought.

There was a man in Cap's truck there that had come to babysit the house. "Harry," Cap said, "stay with her and I'll check with you tonight."

"OK, Cap." Harry said.

"OK, boys, take the van and go on home, I'll see you in a few days."

"OK, Cap," they said. They all got in the van and left.

"Come on, Joe," Cap grinned, "let's go see about some breakfast."

"Man, I'm ready!" I said. We got in Cap's pickup and left the ranch.

Later on when we pulled in Cap's driveway it was good daylight. Betty and Rita were up and waiting for us. As we came in the house, Cap said, "Can a couple of hardworking fellers get something to eat?"

"Sure can, honey," Betty said, as she walked up and kissed him.

Rita gave me a hug and said, "You all right, Joe?"

"Sure, babe, never better," I answered. Then we went in to the table. It wasn't long before breakfast was on the table. "Man, this has been a night!" I said.

"Well, Joe," Cap said, "you made yourself ten thousand tonight."

"Cap," I said, "I sure do appreciate it. You know, this will really help me much more than you could ever know."

"Well, Joe," Cap said, "that's what friends are for, to help each other when they can. And you know me, Joe, if I can't help a man, I sure as hell ain't going to hurt him."

Well, I had to turn away when he said that. I thought, how can I betray this man that has been my friend since boyhood? But then I thought, hell, it's the law; he knows it, he broke it, and that's his problem.

"Well, Cap," I said, "I'm tired out. I think I'll turn in now."

"OK, Joe," Cap said, "sleep good, buddy, you earned it."

I got up and went into the bedroom feeling mighty bad. Rita was there waiting for me, and I soon forgot about everything except her warm kisses and her body next to mine.

CHAPTER EIGHT

The next morning Cap said, "Joe, let's take the girls and run over to the lake. I hear the specks are biting, and I sure would like to have a mess of freshwater fish for a change."

"That sounds good to me, Cap," I said.

We loaded up Betty's car with supplies and groceries. Cap hooked his boat up to the trailer hitch and we took off to Lake Okeechobee for the weekend.

At a fish camp we rented two cabins right on the lake. After we got settled in, we backed the trailer down the boat ramp and launched Cap's boat. It was a nineteen foot open fisherman with plenty of room for all of us. The girls packed us a lunch, and then we got aboard and started out. We fished all morning without a bite. I was discouraged. Then we moved over by the lock in the dike and tried there.

Cap said, "Let's eat some groceries and rest a while. I know where we can probably find them." About 2:00 p.m. we pulled the anchor and started south to the grass flats Cap told us about. Pretty soon we were there and anchored the boat in about four feet of water. We couldn't get any closer because there were tree stumps and grass that would foul the propeller on the outboard.

Betty said, "Cap, Rita and me will stay in the boat, honey."

"OK, baby," Cap said. Then he looked up and turned his head in different directions. "I smell them," he said. "We hit it lucky, Joe."

"How's that, Cap?" I said.

"The specks," Cap said, "they are bedding here and laying their eggs. Come on, Joe, let's go catch some fish." He took his cane pole and a cup of worms and stepped over the side into waist deep water. He waded out about fifteen feet from the boat, baited his hook with an earthworm and threw his line out. Immediately the cork bobber went under and Cap pulled in a speck as big as your hand. He took him off the hook and pulled a string through his mouth and out his gill. Then he tied the string to his belt behind him and dropped the fish in the water.

"Come on in, Joe!" Cap hollered as he caught another fish. I thought, what the heck, and grabbed a pole, stepped out of the boat, and waded over to Cap. After an hour we both had long strings of fish trailing behind us as we moved along the bed and fished. We were really catching those rascals. I'd never seen fish bite like this before.

I was really enjoying myself until I felt my string tugging at my back, and pulling me off balance. "What the hell?" I said and looked behind me. "Jesus, Cap, look at that!" I shouted. Cap laughed and reached over with his pole and smacked about a four foot moccasin on the head. He had the last fish on the string in his mouth and was trying to pull him loose when I felt him pull me back. "I'm gettin' in the boat," I said.

Cap laughed, "I guess we got enough for supper now." As we waded over to the boat I could almost feel that damn snake biting me at anytime. I was sure glad to get to the boat. The snake had followed us all the way to the boat trying to get a fish. We pulled the anchor and started back to the fish camp.

Around dusk we pulled up to the dock and tied up. The girls gathered up the gear and went into Cap's cabin to get supper started. Cap and I took our specks over to the workbench at the end of the dock and started cleaning them. I would scale them and Cap would fillet them. Pretty soon the bugs were driving me crazy. I kept slapping them and cussing. Cap looked at me and said, "You'll beat yourself to death trying to kill skeeters that way. You can't kill them all. Just brush them off like this." He reached up behind his neck and wiped a handful of bloody mosquitoes away.

"Damn, Cap, I don't know how you stand it," I told him. Cap

just smiled and kept on cleaning fish. We finished up and while Cap hosed everything down, I took the pan of fish in to the girls to cook.

Cap and I went into the front room of the cabin and opened ourselves a couple of beers. A little later Betty called out for us to come in to supper. We lost no time getting there. What a meal! Fried fish, hushpuppies, french fries, salad and a cold beer. "Man, this is living, Cap!" I said.

Cap grinned at me and asked Betty to get us another beer. I had never seen Cap drink this much. He was really relaxed. After supper we all went into the front room and sat down.

"You girls let them dishes go, you can get them in the morning. Come over here by me, honey." Cap told Betty.

"Cap," I said, "that damn snake scared the devil out of me; I could just feel him biting me."

"That ol' moccasin didn't mean no harm, Joe." Cap said. "He was just hungry, that's all. Snakes is pretty smart creatures, but moccasins is the smartest of them all. You'd be surprised how smart they are." Cap took another beer out of the cooler and opened it. "I remember one time I was fishing on the bank of a canal with worms. I wasn't having much luck and I was hitting that bottle of Jim Beam pretty hard. Anyway, I heard a frog crying. I looked, and over to my right, at the edge of the water a frog was caught by a moccasin about the same size as that one today. He had his supper for today. Well, I thought, looky here now. This frog is my bait. So I reached down and grabbed that ol' moccasin by the neck and took that frog. I poured a shot of Jim Beam down the snake's throat and threw him back in the water."

"My God, Cap," I said, "that was a dangerous thing to do. You could have been bitten!"

Cap said, "Well, I tell you, Joe, I wasn't feeling no pain that day. I was pretty high. Anyway, I baited my hook with that frog and cast my line out, and went back to fishing. After a while I felt something keep bumping my leg. I looked down, finally, and guess what?"

"What was it, Cap?" Rita and I both asked at the same time.

Cap grinned and took a swallow of his beer, then he said, "It was that moccasin, back with another frog." Then he laughed and took another swallow of his beer.

"Damn, Cap," I said, "you got me that time! I was believing every word you said."

Cap laughed and said, "Don't feel bad son, they caught me on it, is how I learned it."

Rita asked, "Is there any alligators in that lake where you guys were wading around?"

"Full of them," Cap said. I didn't say a word. I was glad to be out of there myself. Cap said, "How about another beer, honey?"

"Sure, baby," Betty said. She went and got another beer for him.

He was sitting there with his head hanging down. He looked up and said, "Gators are interesting critters. I've been around them all my life and I still don't know everything about them."

Rita asked, "Will they catch you, Cap?"

"Well now, Rita, most of the medium sized gators, say up to about seven or eight foot, will leave you alone and most of the time, will try to get away from you if they can. As long as you ain't around their cave."

"What does that mean, 'their cave'?" Rita asked.

Cap said, "It's a hole that the sow gator will dig to nest in. If you look along the canal banks, you can spot where she has been crawling in and out, and dragging herself from the cave. They will dig under the roots of a tree sometimes and the cave might go back fifteen foot from the mouth. Sometimes they will dig one right in the middle of a sawgrass prairie, and you can walk up on it before you know it, if you ain't paying attention. When I was hunting gators for their hides, we'd rod them out of their caves and kill them. That old sow would be madder than hell when she come out."

"What's that mean, 'rod them out'?" Rita asked.

"Well," Cap said, "we take a steel rod about twelve foot long, and about a half inch thick, and sharpen one end of it. Then we push it down in the ground to the cave and prod for the gator. You find the back of the cave, then prod her till she comes out."

"Sometimes a gator will catch you when he is hungry and people have been feeding him. Mostly that happens around a lake somewhere near a town. The gator gets to depend on handouts like that. Sometimes he will catch a dog or he has been known to catch a small child. They lose their fear of man when they have been fed like that."

"In the dry season they will travel across the land hunting water. I remember when Betty and me first got married. We were riding along the road in my pickup, and saw about a six foot gator. He was at the shoulder of the road trying to get to the canal. I pulled over, parked the truck, got out and ran at him. I don't know what in hell I thought I was doing, showing off for Betty, I reckon. Anyway, he turned and crawled off to the palmettos with me hot after him. Well, I caught up with him and he turned around and got up on his four legs hissing, and took out running at me. Man, I got gone, with that gator hot on my tail. He run me plumb to the road before he give up and flopped back down on his belly. Betty was laughing at me, and I got mad at that gator. He was laying there looking at me and I thought, 'I'll learn you to shame me in front of my new wife you son o bitch.' I picked up a lightered knot limb and run in on that gator and beat him to death with it."

"What's a lightered knot limb, Cap?" Rita asked.

Cap said, "It's a pine limb that has layed out on the ground and seasoned till the wood is hard. They make good firewood, and lightered posts make good fences. Anyway, I beat that damn gator to death with it."

"Tell the rest, honey," Betty laughed.

Cap grinned and said, "Why, I cut that gator's tail off with my axe, and we took it home and fried it. Betty loved it, and a gator tail ain't been safe around her since."

"Oh, Cap!" Betty laughed. I looked at Rita and she was laughing so hard there were tears in her eyes. It was a great evening. Everyone was mellow and a little high from the beer. I completely forgot about my job and Cap's occupation. I was having a good time.

Cap said, "Rita, there ain't no end to the things I could tell you about gators. A funny thing happened when I was down in South America. I was visiting a friend of mine in Colombia at his ranch. It was located next to a big lake down there. Everybody was sitting outside taking it easy, and enjoying themselves by the water after noon time. Then some of the ranch hands came up to us with about a five foot cayman. I guess that's what it was, it had a shorter tail than a gator. They all called to me to come see the critter. Well it was just another gator to me. I walked over to look at it. The ranch hands were grinning and poking each other and looking at me. I squatted down by the cayman and told them to turn him over on his back. My amigo told them what I said in Spanish. They looked at each other and thinking me just a crazy gringo, they turned him over on his back. I figured a cayman was no different than a gator, so I reached out and started stroking him from his neck down and across his belly. Pretty soon he started to relax. I kept on stroking him and he went to sleep. I motioned for the men to turn him loose and get back. I just kept on stroking him and then I stood up and stepped back, and he just lay there on him back out like a light. All the men were sure got away with. I sure fooled that bunch! I bumped him with my foot, and he turned over and took off for the lake."

"Cap," I said, "this isn't another moccasin story, is it?"

"No," Cap said, "that really happened like I told you, Joe. You can do the same thing with those little green lizards you see around on the bushes here. It does something to their equilibrium or something. I reckon it would work on any reptile, I don't know."

"It is funny how a gator is. They will dig down in the mud and make holes in the dry season. Minners, crawdads, tadpoles, and snakes all live on account of that gator hole. The whole thing depends, I reckon, on the ol' allygator; he's part of it all."

"I can see that they would be important to the food chain," I said.

"They sure are," Cap said, "but the way them fellers is building and fencing us out, we are all gonna be history pretty soon. The gulf coast fishermen and the wild things too. But you know something, Joe? I was just as bad for the gator myself."

"How's that?" I asked.

Cap said, "Well, that ol' gator made me a living before I ever thought of the pot business."

"How did he do that?" I asked.

Cap said, "The hides, Joe. We would kill them for the hides, and sell them. They brought good money back then. I killed many a gator for his belly."

"Don't you take the whole hide?" I asked.

"No," Cap said, "you just start at the end of his jaw and peel that belly hide off plumb down to his tail. It tans better, and that's all the market there was. Now then the state has got in the gator business. They control it and license the sale of hides, meat, and all."

"But Joe! This country down here has always had to be outside the law to survive. When people first come down here, a lot of them was running from the law. Back then they used to hunt them egret plume birds for their feathers. Then their younguns got grown and Prohibition was in, and they would run rum from Cuba in them little boats about nineteen or twenty feet long. They would bring them back so loaded that they only had about a foot of free board. That took guts in them seas."

"Some of them made moonshine to get by, and a few smuggled Chinese folks in. Mainly, though, they tried to make a living fishing for mullet. Mullet only sold for about half a cent a pound and they could barely make a living at it. They didn't have well boats or outboard motors back then, they had to row their mullet skiffs in a circle around a school of fish. Now with these new boats they can strike and take them in no time. But back in the old days they was a lot of fish, not like now. Now they can't bunch up like they used to. Too many yankee boats running around. About the time you are about ready to strike a run you have been sitting on for hours, one of them fellers will run right through. They don't know no better, Joe."

"The state years ago passed a closed season law that made it against the law to catch mullet or even to have them. That made the price go up and most of the fishermen could catch them and salt them down and smuggle them by the truck load to the markets in Georgia. The law would catch them and put them in jail, but the profit was there and they had no better way to make money, so they kept right on doing it, until they changed the law, and that's taken the profit out of it. You know, Joe, if they done that today, we'd be out of business. Ain't no use smuggling anything if you can't make no money out of it."

Cap reached for his beer and took a long pull. He sat there with the beer in his hand looking down at the floor. Then he said, "Talking about gators, if you was to get in the water around a big one, I guess he'd catch you. I've seen some at least fifteen foot and maybe bigger. A gator that size ain't scared of nothing. I've seen gators lay up on the back of the canal and knock a full grown hog down with his tail."

Cap sat there with his head down and dozed off. Betty got up and took the can of beer from his hand and set it on the table. "Come on Cap, it's time for bed, honey." She pulled him to his feet, and Cap stood there weaving a little and grinning at Rita and me.

"Goodnight, folks, I've about had it," he said. We said goodnight and walked out to our cabin together.

We got up about noon and started getting things together to leave. We were all a little hung over. "How you feeling, Cap?" I asked.

Cap groaned and said, "I feel like I been eating cattails."

Rita laughed and said, "Cat tails? Cap, what's the cats think?"

Cap laughed and said, "Rita, those green long stalks with the round brown ends you see growing along the edge of the canals in fresh water are called cattails."

Rita said, "The ones that look like a hot dog on the end?"

"That's right," Cap said. "It's just an old saying around this country. Maybe you could eat them, I don't know. You can eat a lot of things growing wild in this country, like swamp cabbage. Did you ever eat any swamp cabbage, Rita?"

"No, Cap, I never even heard of it. What is it?"

"It's the heart of a young cabbage tree," Cap said. "Some folks call them Sabal palms. You cut the top part of the tree out and take the heart out and peel the outside layer off. They are called boots. Anyway, you peel the boots off 'till you get to the heart. That is sweet and tender to eat raw, but it is real rich like that. Most folks boil it with plenty of seasoning and fatback and that's fitting to eat, I tell you."

"I've eaten it, Rita," I said, "and let me tell you, it is good."

Betty said, "Rita, when we get home Cap can go cut one and I'll show you how to cook it."

"She can cook it right, too, not bitter at all," Cap said.

I got up and picked up some of the suitcases and went out to the car. Cap hitched the boat up to the trailer hitch on the car while the girls and I finished taking everything out and loading the car. Before long we were ready, and pulled out and headed down to the store to gas up.

We had spent most of the afternoon lounging around and by the time we got on the road it was dark. We got into Snapper Bend about eleven that night. We were all tired and went right to bed, but as tired as I was, Rita and I made love. Later lying there in bed, we talked to each other about our situation.

Rita said, "Joe, let's get out of here. This is getting too personal for me."

"I know it, honey," I said. "I'll tell Cap that we want a place of our own. That will get us out of here where we can move more freely."

"We still have to find Manny and Kim. I wonder where they went to?" Rita said.

"I don't know," I said, "but after that deal at the airboat camp, they have sure laid low. We better get some sleep, baby." Then I leaned over and kissed her goodnight.

Chapter Nine

I woke up about ten o'clock and the girls had breakfast waiting on me. Cap had already eaten and was grinning at me over a cup of coffee.

"How you feeling, Joe?" he said.

"Good, Cap," I said. "I still have to go pick up my things on the other coast, you know. Then maybe me and Rita might get a little place of our own. Not that we don't like it here, but you know how it is."

Cap laughed and said, "We know, Joe, and we wish you the best. I don't think you could find a better girl than Rita."

"Thanks, Cap," I said. "I'll take off in a couple of hours."

"OK," Cap said, "and Joe, I made a couple of calls early. I was out pretty late last night and I guess I'm pretty tired. I'm going back to bed for a while."

"Yeah, Cap, I don't blame you. Rita," I said, "you want to come with me, hon?"

"Yes, Joe," she said, "I'd love to."

I told Cap and Betty we would probably pick up our things later and then we got up to leave. Cap said he might have a little something for me later on when I came back.

I said, "That's fine, Cap, that will get our apartment."

He grinned at me and said, "Ain't it nice, Joe?"

"Sure is, Cap." Then Rita came out of the bedroom. I said, "Rita, let's go look at our apartment."

Rita and I left Cap and Betty, and after checking in on Carl at the substation, we left and rode downtown. We pulled into the parking lot of the Everglades Bar, got out and went inside.

Tina, the barmaid, looked at me and grinned, "Hey, Champ! No more trouble, OK?"

"Tina," I said, "if no one starts anything there won't be any."

"What'll you have?" she asked.

"A Bud for me, what about you, Rita?"

"The same, Hon," she said and squeezed my arm. Tina went down the bar to get our beers and I looked at Rita.

"Hon this, Hon that," I laughed.

"Well, you are my Honey, aren't you?" she said. "I'm supposed to be your girl on this cover, right?"

"Right!" I said, and leaned over and kissed those lips. Then we pulled back, looked at each other and did it again.

"Hey! Come up for air, you two!" laughed Tina, standing there with our beers. She put them down in front of us and walked out from behind the bar to the jukebox. She looked over her shoulder and asked, "Have y'all heard the smugglers song yet?"

"Yeah, I have," I said. "Everybody has heard the Smuggler's Blues."

"No, not that one," she said, "the other one that taxi guy up in Naples wrote. He called it the Smuggler's song. You don't know it? It goes like this," and she sang, "It's Hard to be a Smuggler."

Damn right it is, I thought. Tina dropped a coin in the jukebox and played the song. Rita and I got up to dance and as I held her in my arms and listened to the words, I thought, damn it's true, that song. We finished the dance and returned to the bar. Hearing the front door open I swung around on the stool, and Kim Snell was standing there with a surprised look on his ugly face. He turned and ran back out the door, jumped in the Bronco and tore out of the parking lot. I threw money on the bar, said "see you later, Tina," and we rushed out the door to my pickup and followed him.

Now my pickup had no ordinary motor. This one was hopped up to the max, and would really run on the top end. Well, old Kim hit the Alley, turned right and stepped on the gas. But that Bronco was no match for my pickup. We kept him in sight until he turned off the road. That's when Rita saw what she was riding in. I put the pedal to the metal, as they say, and was on him before he knew it. But even then I was a little late. Kim was pulling out in an airboat.

Again luck was with me. Some unfortunate, trusting soul had tied up his airboat a few feet away, and had even left the key under the seat cushion. I jumped on the boat and found the key. "Wait for me, Rita!" I shouted, and the boat fired right up. It was a hot airboat. I gave it the gas, spun around and took off after Kim. He was running up the old trail and I was right on his tail. The trail ran through and around cypress islands and short prairies of sawgrass, then back in the cypress again. Kim and I had to really watch what we were doing or risk ripping the bottom of the boats out.

Even so, I started gaining on Kim and he tried to shoot at me. That was next to impossible as he had to try to lean outside the airboat so as not to hit his prop. He gave it up and concentrated on trying to outrun me. About that time he sideswiped a cypress knee at the edge of the trail and almost lost control of his boat. By then we were out of the cypress and on the sawgrass. I wanted him alive so I held my fire. We were running flat out in a hot race across the Everglades. I was gradually gaining on him when he started sliding sideways and firing at me. I fired back with my mack eleven, thinking to disable his boat and stop him. I took a glancing shot on my hip just as I opened fire. The impact spun me off balance and I shot his rudders to pieces. Of course, with no control of his boat he couldn't straighten up his slide and he hit a heavy growth of sawgrass. The impact flipped the boat over, dumping him on his head in front of the boat.

He was sitting up, holding his head with both hands when I pulled up beside his boat. Kim looked down the barrel of all that firepower in my hand and he just wilted.

"Come on over here, you jerk," I told him. Kim waded over to my boat, climbed in and sat down in front of me. I pulled the rudders hard over and gave it the gas. The boat spun around and we took off up the trail back to the landing.

Rita came running down to the landing. "You stopped him, Joe!" she said.

"Yeah, baby. He had a little accident with my eleven here." Then I stood up and stepped down off the boat

Rita saw the blood on my side and looked up at me. "Oh Joe, baby, you're hurt!" she cried.

My hip was hurting like hell, but I said, "It's only a bruise, Rita. I can handle it." I turned and looked at old Kim sitting there in the boat.

"Where's Manny, Kim?" I asked.

"He's at the Dogleg camp waiting for me," he said. "I was supposed to be in town for some groceries. But I stopped at the bar and saw you."

"Yeah!" I said. "Gave you quite a shock, huh?"

"Yeah," he said, "with Rita double-crossing Manny and being sweet on you, it did."

"Well Kim, my boy, you are in deep trouble. Come on down here nice and easy now and don't make me have to kill you." He climbed down off the boat, and I said, "Rita, honey, look in my war chest and get me a pair of cuffs out."

"Damn," Kim said, "a cop, you're a damn cop!"

"You got it, kid," I said, "and you have the right to remain silent; anything you say can be used against you . . ."

"I know the rest of that crap," he said.

"Just as long as you know, scumbag," I told him.

Rita cuffed him and said, "Now what?"

"Rita, honey, I want you to take him back to town and tell the watch commander to stick him in a different cell than Carl. I'm going after Manny."

"Be careful, Joe," she said. "I don't want to lose you now that I have found you."

"Don't worry, baby, you won't lose me." I said. Then I walked to her, pulled her in close to me and kissed her until she pushed me back.

She laughed and said, "No more, Joe, or I won't leave." She walked over and opened the door of the Bronco and said, "OK, Kim, get your big lard ass in the seat." Kim walked over and struggled up and in the front seat. Rita strapped him in with the seat belt. Then she went around and got into the driver's seat, blew me a kiss, and headed back to town.

I turned and jumped on the airboat, hit the mag switch and she fired right up. Then I hit the other mag and the motor smoothed right out. I hit the gas, pulled the stick all the way over, spun around, straightened up and then punched the pedal down. This boat could really run. I went up to the long trail by the grass, and then doubled back to the Dogleg. When I hit the canal I let the motor idle. I moved along about like before and slipped right up the canal to the camp.

As before, I tied up, eased out of the boat and waded up through the cypress. I pulled myself up on the catwalk and peeked in the window. Manny and another guy were in the kitchen area with a bale of pot on the table in front of them. It had been cut open and they were putting it in bags. I guess it was a special product, because I couldn't see Manny doing street level business. Over on a chair I could see another bale. Evidently the other man was a buyer's representative, and they were making up samples for him to take.

Both men had guns stuck in their belts, and there was an Uzi on the table. I knew I had to hit them fast, so I stepped in the door and shouted, "Freeze!" They whirled around and Manny reached for the Uzi. The other man was just standing there with his mouth open, staring, when I opened up with the Mac Eleven. I sprayed them across and back, almost cutting them in half. They never had a prayer.

I walked in, looked at the bodies, and said, "Well, Manny old boy, this just ain't your day. It was you or me." They never had a chance.

Later I slid the airboat up to the bank, tied up and got into my pickup and headed back to town. Going straight to Cap's house, I arrived right at supper time. As usual, Betty had a great meal prepared. Fried mullet with grits, fried snook with french fries, hush puppies, sliced tomatoes, and iced tea. I pulled out a chair across from Rita and sat down.

"Cap," I said, "I'll say it again, you sure are a lucky man."

"Yeah, Joe, I sure am!" Cap said. "My house is paid for, Betty has a new car that's paid for, we have a nice boat that's paid for, I got a friend like you . . . what more could a man want?"

"Well, Cap, I'll tell you a little later, but right now it's getting late and I am really tired." Everyone agreed that sleep was a good idea. So after saying good night, Rita and I went to our room and Cap and Betty went to theirs.

About one-thirty in the morning my eyes snapped open, and I was aware of someone standing by the bed. It was Rita. She whispered, "Joe!"

"I'm awake," I told her. The cloud passed by, and in the sudden moonlight she was breathtaking. Her nightgown in a puddle at her feet, she was waiting.

"Like what you see?" she asked.

I just groaned and reached for her. She came to me like a flame. For a few minutes we consumed each other with a burning passion, and as quickly it was over. She lay beside me with her head on my shoulder.

"Joe," she said, "you are the best."

"Rita," I said, "there's more to come." I lay back and smiled in the darkness.

Chapter 10

After breakfast, I asked Cap to come on out to the porch and talk awhile.

"Sure thing, Joe, be right out."

I sat back in the rocker and waited for Cap, and was trying to think what to do when Cap came out and sat down in his rocker.

"What's on your mind, Joe?" Cap asked.

"Well, Cap, I'm worried about that voice. I know I've heard it before, and I think you know who it is."

"Joe," he said, "don't go any further with this. I told you before he's a dangerous man, and I want to protect you. Sometimes I wish I didn't know as much as I do."

"Well Cap, that's OK, forget it, I was just curious," I said. "I've got to run into town for a while. I'll see you later."

"OK, Joe," Cap said, "I'll be here."

I walked to the door and called, "Hey, Rita! Wanta take a ride with me?"

"Sure, Joe," she said, as she came out and took my hand.

As we walked to my pickup Betty said, "Look at that Cap, ain't that sweet?"

"Sure is, honey," said Cap. "Maybe they can have what we do. Couldn't happen to a greater guy."

"I know it," Betty said. "Rita is a sweet girl, too." They stood there together on the porch holding hands and watched us drive off.

We drove straight to the substation, pulled in and parked. In the watch commander's office I said, "Well, I guess it's about time to bring the curtain down on this scene."

The commander said, "Joe, what are you going to do now?"

"Well, sir," I said, "we are going to see Carl and Kim. It's time for the old Mutt and Jeff routine."

Rita laughed and said, "Who's the bad guy, you or me?"

I said, "Well baby, you be nice, and I'll scare the hell out of them."

The watch commander said, "I'll have them brought over and you can use the two offices across the hall. We have them fixed up with two-way mirrors facing another office in back of them."

"OK, commander," I said, "I'm ready when you are." Carl and Kim were brought in and put in separate offices. Rita and I went in to see Carl first. He was sitting there in the chair, handcuffed and looking sullen.

"Carl," I said, "you can help yourself now by telling me everything you know about this smuggling that you are involved in."

"I got nothing to say," replied Carl.

"Well, Carl," I said, "we got a tough prosecutor and he will ask for the max if you don't cooperate. If you are worrying about Manny, he's history. I killed him myself." That got his attention, but he still just sat there with his head down and wouldn't say anything else. "Well, Carl," I said, "think about it and we will be back."

We left and went into the office with Kim Snell. "Snell, as I said before boy, you are in deep trouble."

He said, "Yeah? How deep?"

I said, "Carl is willing to cooperate and testify against you, and he—"

"Hold on," Kim said, "just wait a minute now. That jerk don't know nothing, but I can help you, and I will. Just ask the boys downtown about me. I been working with the Feds for years."

Then I said, "You dumb jerk, who do you think you are talking to? We are the Feds, we are D.E.A., so don't try to bullshit us."

Kim got sorta white around the gills then, and he said, "Man, I can be useful to you, I can give you the big man that runs the whole job. But you got to make it worth my while."

"What else could you give us?" I asked him.

"Well," he said, "I know a lot of people in this business. I could set them up for you. I can't do anything in jail, though. What do you say?"

"Kim, I hate to make deals with scum like you, but I'll think about it for a while." We went back to the commander's office and talked it over.

Rita had gone back and talked to Carl while I questioned Kim and she thought he was about to break.

"Well," I said, "I think we can use Kim to round up a lot of smugglers, so I vote we make a deal with him for his testimony on the higher up people. I'll have to check with my boss. He pretty well trusts my judgment and I see no problem with it."

We had coffee in and I checked with the Bureau Chief. As I thought, there was no problem with the deal with Snell. We would use him in court, then wire him and put him on the street. Of course, I knew that he would smuggle himself and continue to use cocaine and otherwise break the law. But as a would be famous prosecutor once said to a jury, and I quote, "Ladies and Gentlemen, we must use scum like this to catch the smugglers. It's unfortunate but true."

I went back and told Kim, "You got a deal, tramp, but you better not cross us." He swore on his life that he wouldn't. I called for a stenographer and we took his statement. He identified The Voice for me. It was Roy Depeppo. He named Cap and Betty, Manny and Carl, and about ten others involved in the operation. We then went in and told Carl that Kim had given us a statement and he could either cooperate for ten years, or we would see that he got twenty with no parole. Well, old Carl went for it hook, line, and sinker. Now we had enough to go to the grand jury for indictments.

The warrants were out and signed and we were ready. In my report to the home office I 'forgot' to mention the pop-up job I worked on. The raid was set for the next Friday morning. I still hadn't said anything to Cap. I had tried to get him to tell me who the head man was, but he didn't. Anyway, after Kim started playing ball with us, his information wasn't necessary.

I told Rita, "Well, it's out of our hands now, Hon. The task force is in charge now."

"Yes," she smiled, "it's too bad about Cap, Joe."

"Yeah," I said, "but I tried to open the door for him. He chose not to accept it."

Friday morning the raid went off like clockwork. Crack teams hit at dawn all over town. First a heavy banging on the front door, and a sleepy voice saying, wait a minute, then the door was opened and the arrest would proceed.

Unfortunately I was part of the raid team that went to Cap's house. I had gradually moved my own and Rita's personal property out of Cap's house on the pretext of moving into our own apartment. The agent in charge of the team banged on Cap's front door and Cap opened it.

"Freeze!" came the command. "On the floor!" Cap was thrown to the floor and a twelve gauge riot shotgun was stuck to his head. Agents poured into the house and effectively searched every room. I heard Betty scream.

"CAP! What is this!"

"Get out of there!" the agent hollered. "Get out of bed now! Get on the floor! Put your hands back!"

I came into the room and said, "Hey! There's no need of this." He just looked at me and said, regulations, and they are scum anyway, and he put the cuffs on her. Betty lay there in her transparent nightgown and never said another word. I must admit I wasn't too happy with her treatment, but there was nothing I could do.

The team brought Cap and Betty into the dining room and sat them down at the dining room table. The agent in charge ordered one of the female team members to take Betty back into her bedroom and get her properly dressed. Then she was brought back into the dining room and sat back down. They were then told they were under arrest. The charges were read to them: conspiracy to smuggle marijuana into the United States, and of course, there were the usual extra charges that stem from that, there being four in all. Then they were read their rights and told that their home, all contents therein, both vehicles, and Cap's boat were seized; and all bank accounts frozen.

Cap looked at me like he was Christ on the cross, and Betty just sat there with big tears pouring down her cheeks.

Then Cap said, "Joe! You were my friend!"

I looked at him and said, "Well, Cap, if you want to play, you got to pay."

There's not much else to tell.

Rita and I got married and are now in the same department. Cap got thirty years. Betty got ten years, and Roy Depeppo cooperated with us against some people higher up that Snell never heard of. He made a deal for three years in a camp.

I keep thinking about the last thing that I ever heard Cap say. He said, "Thirty pieces of silver, Joe?"

Epilogue

Cap thought to himself as the U.S. Marshalls cuffed his hands behind his back in the courtroom, "How could a man do what Joe has done to me?" The marshalls led him out of the courtroom and down the long hall to the elevator. They stood there and waited in silence. Then the doors opened and they entered, and one of the marshalls pushed the down button. They descended to the basement and were led down a long hallway to another lift that took them up to the marshalls' holding cells.

Cap was put in one of the cells, and his handcuffs were removed. There were two other men in the cell that Cap was in. The cell was about a ten feet square room, with a stainless steel toilet with no seat, and a sink with a water tap on top of that. The cell had two low concrete benches on two side walls and a half wall in front of the toilet. The front of the cells were steel bars facing a hallway that led to two other cells and the marshalls' office. Cap sat down on one of the benches and thought about Betty.

As the day passed more men were brought in from different trials and put in the cells. About fifteen men were now in the cell with Cap. Mostly they were all subdued and quiet. One man asked Cap for a cigarette, and Cap told him that he was sorry, but he didn't smoke. About one-thirty in the afternoon the marshalls passed out box lunches and a carton of juice.

Along about five o'clock several marshalls came in with four plastic boxes, and started pulling out leg chains, waist chains, and handcuffs out on the floor. The marshalls opened up the first cell and took two men out at a time. They handcuffed them in front to a waist chain and then two men were chained together with a leg chain. As the men were chained up they were put back in the cell to wait.

After about forty-five minutes they were led out to the elevator. All the men soon learned to shuffle their feet to keep from tripping each other with the leg chains. Cap wondered how in the world he could do thirty years of this. Four or six men were put in the lift and taken to the basement garage. Once there they were lined up and stood waiting for the other prisoners to be brought down.

After a while all the men were brought down. The marshalls were all standing at different points with machine guns and riot guns at the ready. Cap looked at them and thought, "They are really into this scene. They would kill you." Then they were led out to be loaded on the bus. The line of men awkwardly started shuffling to the street where the bus waited. Two at a time, one ahead of the other, they made it up the steep steps of the bus and went to sit in seats behind the steel mesh security screen. Two marshalls got on and locked the security screen door. The bus pulled out and headed for the prison outside the city.

On the outskirts of Miami, the bus arrived at the federal prison. It pulled up to the main building entrance and stopped. The guards got out and one went into the building. Looking out of the window of the prison bus, Cap stared at the double rows of chain link fence that is topped and filled between the fences with razor wire. After a while, a couple more guards game out of the building armed with automatic weapons and took positions a short distance in front and back of the prison bus. A small pickup truck had parked off to the side, and that guard had been there all along with his riot gun held at the ready. Cap thought, "Man, these guys don't take any chances."

The prisoners awkwardly got off the bus and shuffled upstairs and into the building where they were herded into holding cells. After thirty or forty minutes they were moved out two at a time and their chains and shackles were removed. Then they were moved into a hallway where they were told to remove all their clothes. Standing there, naked as the day they were born, a guard told them to shake their fingers through their hair, show him the bottoms of their feet, their hands, all body orifices, and more dehumanizing procedures. Then they were moved up the hallway and issued underwear, coveralls, cheap slip-on tennis shoes, and put in another holding cell.

Eventually, after they were processed through mug shots and fingerprinting and more paperwork, they were led into a maximum unit to be fed and locked down for the night. Laying down on his bunk, Cap finally drifted off to sleep. Deep in the night, Cap dreamed he was with Betty on his airboat, sliding fast across the grass in his beautiful Everglades.

Smuggler's Song

It's hard to be a smuggler
The whole world's after you
That good old boy you trusted
Was undercover blue.

Your best friend just got busted
The one you thought was true
The one you'd give your life for
Has gone and rolled on you

It's hard to be an outlaw
And walk that smuggler's trail
The judge thinks that you are rich
And sets a real high bail

Then you call the local bondsman
He's your friend tried and true
And when he finally gets you out
He owns the rest of you

Then you go and hire a lawyer
You're standing there in tears
They all said he was the best
He only got you thirty years

You just look at him in sadness
Man, that's a real raw deal
He said, Son give me five more grand
We'll just file us an appeal

Yes, it's hard to be an outlaw
And pass that smuggler's test
Just when you think you've beat that game
Here comes the I.R.S.

Yes, it's hard to be an outlaw
So hear this smuggler's tale
Don't you try to be a smuggler
It's hard here in this jail

TIME IN RHYME

I Remember All

I can still recall
Little boy of ten
Hearing mothers call
Hound dog loving him

I remember then
Old worn foot log
Calling his best friend
King the champion dog

Walking a green field
That stream flowing through
Standing still whistles shrill
Hollers I hear you

Darkness coming on
Flying like the wind
Running right along
Lop eared hound with him

No supper on the table
Dad is looking mad
Seems he is never able
To keep from being bad

Little boy of ten
Thinking life is hard
Seeing his best friend
Banished to the yard

Happiness is gone
There is only gloom
Hungry and alone
Sobbing in his room

Then a friendly sound
Thumping on the floor
A miracle is found
Crawling through his door

Mothers little man
Smiling now instead
A tender loving hand
Seeing he is fed

A tired little boy
Hound beneath his bed
Asleep in silent joy
Sweet dreams in his head

I remember all
A little boy of ten
Hearing mothers call
Hound dog loving him

I can still recall
I remember all

The Mixing Pot

Thinking back along the years
Of accidents and childish tears
My happiest day of the lot
When mother baked I licked the pot

Mother was my dearest friend
Pausing I remember when
She would call and like a shot
I would run to lick the pot

The wisdom mother gave to me
That only time has made me see
Tender message a small child got
Love is icing on the pot

Mother told me of a throne
Of a journey made alone
Of a Sun shining hot
On a golden mixing pot

She was my teacher and my way
To value's that I hold today
Teaching love and hating not
God is love the mixing pot

White Falling rain

White falling rain
Turning to snow
Cycles of living
Blue water flow

Precipitation
Drops in the air
Falls on the mountain
Streams everywhere

Running together
Joining to grow
Forming the rivers
Oceans below

Now self destruction
Toxic food chains
Careless production
Chemical rains

Nature is crying
Bad water dreams
Blue lakes are dying
Rivers and streams

Air land and water
All dying away
Mankind is killing
His world today

Everyone listen
Think and refrain
We must return to
White falling rain

Earth water rising
Restoring the same
Life giving cycle
White falling rain

Hooked

First they get your money there
And that will be a lot
It's what they do everywhere
And it's every cent you've got

Then they come to your home
Swear they will be true
Say you are not alone
They will be there for you

With one finger of a hand
They now control your mind
Their powers all across the land
Now you have bought their line

It was done so easy
With just a finger crooked
Now it's a necessity
You know that you are hooked

You payed them from the start
You need them everyday
You know they have no heart
And you must always pay

Now they have the power
You know that must be wrong
But you count each hour
Now that you are alone

Now you really need them
But they cannot be found
You know you can never win
And they have let you down

Then you try to give them up
But that cannot be done
their evil line cannot be cut
You know that they have won

Please my friend if you have the time
In your travels all about
Get those people on the line
Tell them my phone is out

I Had A Dream Last Night

I had a dream last night
In my prison cell
Lord it was an awful sight
I dreamed I was in hell

Burning there with the dead
Flames leaping higher
Hearing screams in my head
My soul was on fire

Misery and pain there
Sorrow and grief
Tortured souls everywhere
Begging for relief

Then my terror grew
The devil looked at me
Lord then I cried for you
To come and set me free

Then I saw a brilliant light
Brighter than hells glare
A blinding force split the night
To face the devil there

Then began a conflict there
Where to my mortal mind
Nothing ever could compare
Not in space or time

Like a million star burst
From the depths of hell
Sounds across the universe
When the devil fell

In my dream last night
In my prison cell
My God won a mighty fight
With satan down in hell

Beneath A Bridge

Once he knelt before a queen
Traveled every point between
Owned executive prestige
Now there's life beneath a bridge

Tread life's greatest pinnacle
Tasted deeply from the well
Dined on golden partridge
Eating now beneath a bridge

Had a trusting view of all
Then a speeding flying fall
Like a well spent cartridge
Lying now beneath a bridge

Mistakes made along the way
Trusting those he won't today
Blindly walked the highest ridge
Reflecting now beneath a bridge

Walked that edge for a look
Prison for the chance he took
Packing box from a fridge
Simple home beneath a bridge

Christ's betrayer's spirit lives
Every time a Judas gives
Freedom now a privilege
Better off beneath a bridge

TIME TO SMELL THE FLOWERS

Life floats away
Like an ocean swell
Flowers bloom today
I can never smell

I live the years
Counting the hours
Old man in tears
Let me smell the flowers

Gray walls I see
Misery I feel
Closing in on me
Gray walls of steel

Lord let me FREE
To feel aprils showers
To gaze upon the sea
To smell the pretty flowers

Let me see the trees
Beyond walls and towers
Green grass and honeybees
Let me smell the flowers

Prison fades away
With you in my mind
My spirit doesn't stay
My body's doing time

Blue skies I see
Gods love I feel
Parting for me
Gray walls of steel

My God above
Almighty powers
Please give me love
Let me smell the flowers

Try Your Time With Jesus

Try your time with Jesus
You have tried it with the sword
Read his word with us
And trust in the Lord

I know it is hard in prison
But he is with you every day
God will help you fight that sin
All you have to do is pray

Jesus is your friend
Only hear His call
You can be with Him
Behind those prison walls

He offers would you please
Just follow in His way
Get down on your knees
Open up and pray

Give your life up to Him
Feel His love enfold
Feel His Holy power when
God receives your soul

HE will fairly judge you
Before His pardon board
So try your time with Jesus
You've tried it with the sword

My Fathers Son

My family wept I was kept
Locked in prison here
I will lose my youthful step
Time will rob each year

Mind and senses reeling
With this heavy load
Who could know the feeling
That never walked this road

Busted tried and locked away
Years before I'm free
I have no other hope today
Time has conquered me

But a presence in my mind
My heart has made me see
There is another doing time
Who walks along with me

He is with me every day
My heart has let him in
He is the only way
I can be free again

He will always care
My soul he has won
He is everywhere
He is my fathers son

Ode To A Wild Girl

To think that I will soon be gone
I thought I had it made
I am young and I was strong
Now I'm dying here with AID's

In this hospital bed all alone
Reflecting on my past
How the life I lived was wrong
Now I know that I can't last

My friends and I would dance and sing
I was drinking whiskey then
I remember I was just fifteen
I took my first drink of gin

A school friend said here's a thrill
And I didn't want to be rude
When he said here take this pill
And he handed me a qualude

I thought he was sharp and wise
When he said look what I got
Try this baby on for size
And I took that acid dot

At first I only sniffed that coke
I never thought that it would kill
Then I sold my body when I was broke
So I could buy another thrill

Booze will ruin your liver
Drugs will fry your brain
But no one lives forever
You can't make it on cocaine

Now we are always together
But it's smack instead of crack
He'll be with me forever now
He's that monkey on my back

No one can live your life for you
But drugs have sure killed me
But I know one thing that's true
Dirty needles are not free

My last word I leave for all
My life will soon be through
See my picture on your wall
I'm dead at twenty two

Jailhouse Millionaires

Behind gray walls of prison
Where no one wants to be
The only guilty one in here
I believe is me

Many men have told me
About how they were framed
That they were never guilty
Just the ones they named

I hear all the stories
All the wealth they had
No one ever was at fault
Just good luck turning bad

They are here in prison
With freedom on their mind
Someone on the out side
Should be inside doing time

Don't tell me your stories
Tell someone who cares
I don't have no money
For jail house millionaires

Muzzle Flashes In The Dark

Kids at play in central park
Muzzle flashes in the dark
On the ground a dying narc
Muzzle flashes in the dark

Uncle please a brand new part
No more drugs to break our heart
No more wars we need to start
No more dying in the dark

If no money who would make
Wasted lives in their wake
Smugglers know the chance they take
Drugs are sold for profits sake

If no drugs for dogs to smell
If no snitch who would tell
If no one to put in jail
If no profit who would sell

If your man has put the blame
On anyone who fits the frame
He just has to say a name
Only money is his game

Dopers dealers baby boys
Killing with their grown-up toys
Making all their deadly noise
Never knowing children's joys

Ruined lives against the wall
Free drugs given to them all
Only then will profits fall
No more dealers left to call

Parents grief of children gone
Calling out their lonely song
Hollow eyed and all alone
Finished lives and ruined homes

Kids at play in central park
Muzzle flashes in the dark
On the ground a dying narc
Muzzle flashes in the dark

So Wrong

Lord hear my plea
Have mercy on me
Look where I fell
A small prison cell

It's starting again
Another night when
Time is so long
I was so wrong

Robbing and stealing
Showing no feeling
Gun in my hand
Big macho man

Smarter than all
Warrior out law
They won't stop me
My destiny

Looking I see
Law chasing me
Strong ghetto child
Running so wild

Knowing my fate
Feeling their hate
Shooting me down
Blood on the ground

I heard that day
My jury say
Crime must not pay
Lock him away

I crossed the line
Bought my own time
Another sad song
Lord I was wrong

Another night then
Praying again
Lord hear my plea
Have mercy on me

Big Time

I wonder girl of you out there
Knowing I am here
I wonder if you still might care
Or ever shed a tear

Remembering how I lost you girl
I was racing to the top
Only greed was my world
I just could not stop

I can still hear you say
You didn't have the time
I stood and watched you walk away
When I crossed the line

Please forgive me if you can
I was never mean
I was just a desperate man
Going for the green

Bars of steel holding me
As I dream of you
I wonder now where you will be
When my time is through

I findly made the big time
Now I plainly see
Doing time for my crime
Big time killing me

TIME

Time is only just a thing
Never ever has been seen
Everyone has time
Until it ends

But a simple truth is sure
Time itself alone is pure
Time is only here
Until it ends

Time behind is only dead
Future time is still ahead
Time is there for you
Until it ends

Time is joy time is pain
Shining sun or cloudy rain
A beginning moving on
Until it ends

Time is precious to us all
Holds us up or lets us fall
Passing fast or slow
Until it ends

Time belongs to you alone
Then your time on earth is gone
Time is just a thing
Until it ends

Everglades Outlaw Man

The government created a park one day
To protect all the wildlife down our way
They saw that land was beautiful, wild, & free
Then they passed laws to keep it from you and me

Then they brought in rangers
To take folks in there so they could see
Heck I've got a boat
Why didn't they hire me

There was some folks in our town
Thought that park was good
But it messed up our fishing
Like we knew it would

Well sir the folks that live in this town
All fished that park up and down
They made their living fishing that way
But the park was closed to fisherman one day

Then they tried fishing north
But that just wouldn't do
Between the tincanners and out boards
The fish were dam few

Well some sold their boats
And they just looked around
Some found low paying jobs
Far away from our town

Well some just gave up
They just hung around and groaned
When them government fellers made that park
Our good old free life was gone

Then one day a man came back to town
He was a fisherman by trade
And he brought home
Smuggling to the Everglades

There was some that didn't like him
And said he was no good
But they all made money
Just like he said they would

Yes sir he helped a lot of folks
His heart was always true
He always said if I can't help you
I'll never hurt you

He knew his business all right
He brought the loads in night after night
Yes he knew that country all the creeks by name
And he was the best in the smuggling game

Well he loved the ladies
And he loved the wine he always said
Bait that trap with a sweet thing
And you'll catch me every time

Yes he made a lot of money
And he had a lot of girls
And he was a king
In the smuggling world

Then one day they tried to trick him
Tried to hire on some spies
But he'd just sit and stare at them
With those big old hound dog eyes

One night they thought he'd be easy to find
But that old boy knew his trade
Hell man they couldn't catch him
That boy was born in the Everglades

Then they subpoenaed him to court
They smiled and said everything just grand
When they called his name a guy stood up
They had subpoenaed the wrong man

Well then they laid low
With their hidden cameras and suck
They watched him above and below
But he didn't care much

They just couldn't catch him
No matter how hard they tried
So they thought we'll just arrest him any way
Everyone knows the law never lies

When they had all the papers ready
They were gonna get him anyway
That man was called to glory
He went home to Jesus on that very day

Yes sir he was the only man I ever knew
Who beat that smugglers game
Captain Buddy—well whatever
Was that mans name

Easy Money M. A.

Boys I drive an eighteen wheeler
Some loads I haul don't pay
But a guy I met from Florida
Said he knew a easy way

So I met him in Miami
I backed up to my load
He gave me that easy money
I pulled out on the road

I guess I just wasn't thinking
I thought this was a easy run
Down the road a blue light was blinking
And I realized what I'd done

Now I know that this ain't right
Why did I make this crazy deal
My hands are sweating and my throat is tight
And I fight this fear I feel

So I'm driving slow and straight
Both hands on the wheel
Now I know the chance I take
Man this takes nerves of steel

Chorus Lord I'm rolling down the freeway
With a trailer load of pot
Thinking everybody out there
Just knows what I got

Man won't it ever change this red light
I feel like a coon up a tree
In plain sight waiting on my right
Is the law looking at me

When that man looks at me
I just know he can read my mind
My breath gives out and I can see
I ain't the outlaw kind

There's a sign ahead in my lights
And it says weight station closed
I know that luck rides with me tonight
But the sweat still wets my clothes

Yeah this run is my first and last
Maybe I might win
Easy money my ass
Lord I'll never run pot again

A Little Bit Of Heaven

Rode on the long chain
Handcuffs and hate
Hit a coed prison
In the bluegrass state

Feeling like a trophy
Standing on display
Lovely ladies asking
How are you today

Smiling and flirting
Wanting me to go
For a walk just to talk
How could I say no

Looking and not touching
Walking in the yard
Prison regulations
Everything is hard

Fast talking ladies
Telling you they care
Talk to me honey
I have time to spare

So many women
Everywhere I see
Boys and girls together
Wishing we were free

Wild coed prison
How can I tell
A little bit of heaven
In this piece of hell

Two Outlaws Together

He's a south Florida outlaw
A bad boy they say
Always loved the ladies
Then he walked away

She's a Dallas desperado
Blue eyed Texas girl
Two outlaws together
In a coed prison world

It's a desperate situation
They are falling hard
Walking slow and talking
Watching for a guard

Two outlaws in prison
Hearing natures call
Fighting off the feeling
But wanting it all

Facing love together
Both afraid to try
Looking and still knowing
Life is slipping by

They have found each other
In a prison world
A lonely Florida outlaw
And a lovely Texas girl

Robert V. Griffin

Hey Remember Me

Hey remember me
Old love me till you die
Are you still riding free
Behind some other guy

Can't you remember me
Remember how to write
Remember when I was free
And riding in the night

You said I was neat
And you sure would like
To put your buns on the seat
Of my old Harley bike

All the fun we had
Could you have forgot
All the times you were glad
We scored a little pot

Man did we have fun
What a happy sight
When we made that orphan run
On that Christmas night

Remember all the boys
And old Frankenstein
Passing out Christmas toys
Now he's doing time

Remember crazy Carol
Dumb as a brick
Loved old weird Harold
What a far out chick

Friendly Fred is gone
Remember that time
Hit a simi head on
Crossed the center line

Remember the lid you hid
The Fed's found it all
Don't you sweat it kid
I said I'll take the fall

You called me old shake & bake
Your lover when I fell
Remember me my name is Jake
And it's Christmas here in hell

Robert V. Griffin

Conspiracy In Insanity

I just wish that I were free
But if you were to ask me
You could never know my view's
Unless you walked in my shoes

But I will try to explain
America has gone insane
All across society
Are victims of conspiracy

If drug conspiracy is your crime
You will do mandatory time
I am a victim too you see
That mythical drug war got me

Now I am doing time
A boat of pot alleged as mine
My sentence states no parole
Child molesters come and go

But razor wire is now behind
Now there is just a line
No chains or shackles on me since
I was back behind the fence

They need no fence to stop me when
My mind will only keep me in
If I stumble and I fall
I go back behind the wall

Here it's peaceful but controlled
Lovely sunsets to behold
Abundant wildlife abounds
Freely run these prison grounds

Life in a restricted world
We walk talk or feed a squirrel
But we have keepers in here too
Who oversee this human zoo

Such a waste of human skill
Victims of an overkill
Conspiracy law never fails
America leads the world in jails

Legalization is the name
Take the profit from the game
Educate the people too
Then this useless war is through

Traveling Soul

I want to live
Judas it's true
I should not give
My life for you

Stool pidgin song
Lying for gold
I stand alone
My freedom sold

Judge sentenced me
Death I am told
There is no mercy
Justice is cold

My savior see's
Day after day
Down on my knees
In faith I pray

Lord make me strong
Humbly I kneel
Convicted wrong
Lost my appeal

I hear the clock
Steps on the floor
Key in the lock
Open cell door

My time is here
I hear them talk
I fight the fear
Last lonely walk

Small silent room
Deadly oak chair
I see my doom
Facing me there

No last reprieve
They're killing again
But Lord I believe
With you I will win

Now I am gone
Leaving the old
Still moving on
A traveling soul

Head Up High

Hold your head up high
Look men in the eye
Know then you can
Be a stand up man

Keep your values strong
Time will pass along
Until that final day
Your chains drop away

No one made you lie
They no longer try
Forget those behind
No one bent your mind

You did time to win
Stood up to the end
You know you have won
Walk out to the sun

Good bye Head Up High
A convict passing by
You paid for your sin
Go on home my friend